DEFENDERS

PAUL MAY

CORGI YEARLING BOOKS

DEFENDERS
A CORGI YEARLING BOOK : 0 440 864429

First publication in Great Britain

PRINTING HISTORY
Corgi Yearling edition published 2001

1 3 5 7 9 10 8 6 4 2

Set in 13/15pt New Century Schoolbook by
Phoenix Typesetting, Ilkley, West Yorkshire

Corgi Yearling Books are published by Transworld Publishers,
61–63 Uxbridge Road, London W5 5SA,
a division of The Random House Group Ltd,
in Australia by Random House Australia (Pty) Ltd,
20 Alfred Street, Milsons Point, Sydney, NSW 2061, Australia,
in New Zealand by Random House New Zealand Ltd,
18 Poland Road, Glenfield, Auckland 10, New Zealand
and in South Africa by Random House (Pty) Ltd,
Endulini, 5a Jubilee Road, Parktown 2193, South Africa.

Made and printed in Great Britain by
Cox & Wyman Ltd, Reading, Berkshire.

For my mother and father

CHAPTER 1

It was the quarter-final of the Cup. Chris Jackson sidestepped a clumsy challenge and the goal was in front of him. There was loads of time. He picked his spot.

'Man on!'

Gary was screaming at him, waving. 'Square ball, Chris!'

Chris ignored him. One more touch, and then he'd blast it. He looked up, and a defender whipped the ball away from his feet.

'Where did he come from?' said Chris.

'You should have passed,' complained Gary. 'I was totally unmarked. You must have heard me shout.'

'Wake up, Parkside!' yelled Mr Shepherd

from the touchline. 'Come on, lads, mark up! Get back and help out.'

Chris started to run. As he crossed the halfway line he heard his dad.

'That'll do, Chris. You're the striker.'

He stopped. Dad was right. Not a lot of point him being back on the edge of his own penalty area. Gary had raced back. He was buzzing around the Cedar Road attackers, trying to nick the ball.

'Chris!' called Mr Shepherd. 'Mark up!'

Chris changed his mind. Maybe I should get back, he thought. He started to move, but as he ran, he saw Jez Wright pull off a brilliant save. Chris waved both arms in the air and yelled.

'To me! To me!'

Jez belted the ball up the field. Chris controlled it and turned. He pushed the ball past a defender and he was away. He took the ball to the edge of the area, then he lashed it past the keeper. He pulled his black and white shirt over his head and swooped towards the watching kids with his arms outstretched.

'OK, Chris,' shouted Mr Shepherd. 'That's enough.'

Chris walked back to the centre circle. He waved to Dad. Mr Shepherd yelled again.

'Concentrate! Come on!'

'Nice one,' said Gary.

'You'd think we'd let one in, not scored,' said Chris. 'What does it take to make him smile?'

'Another goal?' said Gary. 'Look.' He nodded towards the touchline. Mr Shepherd was tapping his fingers to his head.

'He thinks he's managing England,' Chris laughed, as the whistle blew.

Mr Shepherd was the new PE teacher at Parkside Middle School. They had come back after half-term and Mr Grayson, the head-teacher, had announced in assembly that Mr Reddy had been taken ill.

'Mr Reddy won't be back, I'm afraid,' Mr Shepherd told them later in PE, 'so you'll have to make do with me.'

Chris glanced over to the touchline. Mr Shepherd was wiping his glasses on his tracksuit. He made a note on his clipboard. This was his first job and he was taking it very seriously. Chris hadn't seen him smile once.

Cedar Road were pushing forward again. A neat passing movement gave their striker a chance. Chris watched from the halfway line as Kevin Spicer hurled himself, feet first, towards the ball. The Cedar Road striker was cool. He side-footed the ball past

Jez and into the net an instant before Kevin clattered him to the ground. The striker climbed painfully to his feet, but Kevin stayed down. Mr Shepherd ran onto the pitch and examined Kevin's injured leg. When he finally stood up the worry on his face had turned to anger.

'You're lucky,' he said. 'A challenge like that could have done some serious damage. To both of you. As it is you'll need to see a doctor, but I expect a couple of months' rest will see you as good as new.'

'Months!' said Chris. 'But he's our best defender.'

'He's our *only* defender,' muttered Gary.

'If we had a little more discipline in this team,' said Mr Shepherd grimly, 'this wouldn't have happened. Ranjiv will take Kevin's place.'

Gary kicked off. Chris didn't mess about. He swerved round Cedar Road's limping striker and headed for goal. Mr Shepherd obviously thought they were rubbish. Well, maybe some of the others were, but not him. He beat another player and he saw Gary running into space beside him. He didn't need Gary. He didn't need Andy, or Phil, or Ranjiv either. They could call for the ball all

10

they liked. He heard Dad yelling him on, and Mr Shepherd was screaming something too. There was only one defender to beat. Chris swayed to the right and he saw the defender start to commit himself. This was it! A classy flick with his left foot to impress Mr Shepherd and . . .

. . . Chris hit the ground with a thud that knocked the breath out of him. The defender was moving smoothly away with the ball at his feet. He hit a long pass forward. Only Pete was back in defence. He went to control the ball but it bounced away from him, looping into the path of the Cedar Road striker. The striker hit the ball on the volley and the shot crashed against the crossbar as the half-time whistle blew.

'You're a pain in the neck, you are,' said Pete, as they walked off the pitch. 'If you ever passed it, we'd be thrashing them. They nearly scored then.'

'Oh yeah. And whose fault was that? You call that controlling the ball?'

'You're the one who lost it. Gary would have scored, easy. Wouldn't you, Gary?'

Gary was Chris's best mate. He'd always been Chris's best mate.

'I don't know,' he said. 'Maybe.' Chris looked at him.

'Right,' said Mr Shepherd. 'That was a fiasco. And arguing about it isn't going to help. Some of you clearly have a reputation in this school as brilliant footballers. Mr Reddy picked this team before his sudden departure. You lot have just thirty minutes to convince me I shouldn't start again from scratch with a whole new squad.'

'We'll be all right,' said Chris. 'If they clear it properly, I'll whack it in. I was unlucky, that's all.' Pete muttered something, but Mr Shepherd cut him off.

'Let's get one or two things straight,' he said. 'This isn't the perfect moment, but never mind. As far as I can see, your record last season was: won two, lost twelve. Am I right?

There were reluctant nods from the team. Mr Shepherd consulted his notebook.

'You scored twenty-three goals, but you conceded fifty-one. Goodness only knows how you've got this far in the Cup . . .' Chris caught Gary's eye. They both grinned. They both knew how they'd got this far – it was pure luck. A fluky own goal in the first round, and a useless stand-in goalkeeper in the second. Mr Shepherd was still talking.

'If we don't sort a few things out, you won't be going any further. Just do one thing for me, will you? All of you. Try passing the ball. And you, Chris. Wipe that stupid grin off your face.'

'Why's he picking on me?' thought Chris. 'He could have picked on any of them.'

'Pass the ball!' Mr Shepherd called after them, as they walked back onto the pitch.

'Pass the ball . . . pass the ball,' Chris grumbled as he prepared to kick off.

'Well, it wouldn't hurt, would it?' said Gary.

'Oh, come on!' said Chris. 'Not you as well. Who scores all the goals around here? How many did you score last season?'

The ref blew his whistle.

'Here you are then,' said Chris, tapping the ball to Gary. Gary hit it back to Pete, who surprised everyone by stopping it dead. Then he belted it forward. Parkside's luck had changed. The ball hit a defender on the side of the head and ricocheted straight to Chris's feet.

'Give it to Gary!' yelled Mr Shepherd.

Chris looked up and saw Gary's arms waving on the far side of the area. He made as if to pass, then swerved to one side and fired off a powerful drive, across the face of the keeper and into the far corner. He was about to start his celebration routine when he caught sight of Mr Shepherd, shaking his head and turning away. Anyone would think he didn't want to win.

'Thanks, Gazza,' he said. 'That really fooled them. Brilliant run.'

'Yeah,' said Gary. 'Right. Great goal.'

'Nice one, Chris!' yelled Dad from the touchline. 'Let's have a couple more!'

Chris looked at Gary. Gary didn't sound too pleased, but now he was off, chasing back and winning the ball. Chris shook his head. He jogged along the halfway line, waiting for the next clearance. It never came. Cedar Road hit the post twice, and the crossbar once. They would have had a penalty too, if the ref had been looking. They should have won, but they didn't. Instead, Parkside won the game 2–1. They were through to the semi-final of the Cup.

'What's your problem?' said Chris to Gary as they walked out of school. Gary looked at him.

'If you don't know, there's not a lot of point telling you,' he said.

'Oh, come on, Gary, we're mates, right? I'm a striker. You know that. When I get a sight of goal I have to go for it.'

'Yeah, sure,' said Gary. 'Look, I got things

14

to do, OK? I'll see you in the morning.'

'We won, didn't we?' Chris yelled after him. 'Don't you want a lift?' But Gary was gone. A sleek red car pulled up alongside and the door opened.

'Great goals, Chris. Didn't think much of the new coach though. Not exactly a bundle of laughs, is he?'

'Where'd you get this from?' said Chris.

'I treated myself,' said Dad. 'I've got a new job. Got to get the image right.'

'What new job? You didn't say anything.'

'I didn't know for sure. I start in a couple of weeks.' Dad paused. 'The thing is, Chris, the job's in London.'

'In London!'

'Look, I know it's sudden, but I couldn't turn it down, Chris. I'm moving on Saturday.'

Chris sat in silence. London was where Mandy was. Dad's so-called girlfriend. London was two hundred miles away. As long as Mandy had been in London and Dad had been living here in Matfield, Chris had felt safe. He could pretend to himself that everything was OK. Dad lived in a different house, but one day, probably, him and Mum would get back together. Now this.

'Mum hasn't said anything.'

'I haven't told her yet.'

'Oh, great. So I have to pretend I don't know. Like I have to pretend you don't come and watch me play football.'

'It'd only upset Sarah. You know it would.' Sarah was Chris's big sister.

'I told you, Dad. You don't have to come.'

'Look, Chris, you're upset. That's fair enough. But I'll make it up to you. I know London's a long way, but maybe we could go and watch Tottenham, or Chelsea? What about that?'

'Oh, yeah? Like we've been going to go and watch United for the last three years?'

Dad drove in silence for a few moments.

'Well, anyway,' he said, 'I'll still come and watch you play. As often as I can. I've always managed that, haven't I?'

They stopped on the corner of Raidon Street. Chris opened his door.

'Why bother?' he said. 'I don't care if you never come.'

Chris slammed the door and walked away. He heard Dad yelling after him, but he ignored him. His eyes were stinging and his face felt hot. He walked through the overgrown garden of No 28 and opened the front door. Mum was waiting for him. There was a brown envelope in her hand.

'Two—one,' said Chris, chucking his bag onto the floor by the washing-machine. 'It was a walkover. And I scored both goals.'

'Sit down, Chris,' said Mum. 'Sarah, go and get on with your homework.'

'They were good goals, Mum. You . . .'

'Shut up, Chris. Just sit down.' Sarah slipped out of the door.

'You promised me,' said Mum. 'You said this term would be different. And then I get this. Look at it.'

She pushed the letter across the table.

'Dear Mrs Jackson,
We felt you would want to know that
Chris's work, and in particular his home-
work, has not been up to the required
standard this term . . .'

The letter went on, but Chris didn't need to read it.

'You said you'd done your homework. You promised. I can't handle all this, Chris. I've had enough. Either your work improves, or I take the plug off that flaming computer. I told him not to buy it for you. And I'll stop the football too. Don't look at me like that. I mean it, Chris.'

Chris went to his room and flung himself

down on his bed. He stared up at the pictures of strikers that covered the ceiling. They covered the walls too, every centimetre. Chris had never had any doubt about what he was going to be when he grew up. The first thing he could remember doing was kicking a ball at his dad. It had always been the same, Dad in goal and Chris the striker. He closed his eyes and tried to shut out all the bad things. He thought about his goals. They'd been excellent.

'Chris!' Mum's yell broke into Chris's thoughts. 'Are you doing your homework?'

He shut his eyes again, but it was no good. The magic had gone. He got up and pulled the dog-eared folder out of his bag. He looked at what was left of his homework diary. He couldn't read what he'd written. He threw the book on the floor, with the piles of football magazines.

I'm sick of it, Chris thought. I'm sick of it all. He switched on the computer and loaded his new football game. He could sort out the homework tomorrow.

CHAPTER 2

The next morning Chris looked for Gary in the playground before school.

'All right?' he said.

'I was fed up, OK?' said Gary. 'That second goal should have been mine.'

'But you might have missed,' said Chris. 'And I . . .'

'Forget it,' said Gary. 'They were great goals. Brilliant.'

'Yeah,' Chris grinned, remembering. 'Hey, Gary, you know the homework we had last night?'

'The maths, you mean?'

'Oh. That's what it was.'

'Haven't you done it?'

'Can I copy yours? I'll make a few mistakes. I'll make it look good.'

Gary sighed and rummaged in his bag for the book.

'Just don't make it obvious, OK?'

They were still standing there when the new kid arrived. Chris was leaning his book against the wall. He was having trouble keeping the numbers in the little squares.

'Excuse me.'

Chris's pen slipped across the page leaving an ugly black trail. He looked round, expecting to see a teacher. Instead, he saw a tall man with a pony-tail and smiling eyes. Beside the man was a boy. The man was looking at the two maths books in Chris's hands.

'You're nicked!' he said. Chris snapped the books shut.

'Only kidding,' grinned the man.

'Shut up, Dad,' said the boy. He was about Chris's age and height, and thin like his dad. 'Don't worry about him,' he went on. 'He can't help it. We're looking for the office.'

'Straight in through the main door, and turn left,' said Chris. The tall man and the boy walked off across the car park.

'He's wearing a Matfield Town scarf,' said Gary. 'What a dweeb.'

'It might not be,' said Chris, 'Maybe he just likes the colours.'

'Nobody likes purple and orange.'

'Here's your maths book,' said Chris. 'Thanks.'

The new boy's name was Joe Rawson. Mr Grayson brought him in while Miss Jones was doing the register.

'Another one for you, Miss Jones,' he said brightly, surveying the crowded classroom.

'But . . .'

'I'm sure you'll fit him in somehow.' Mr Grayson vanished. Joe was left standing next to Miss Jones's desk.

'There you are, Joe,' she said, pointing to a space next to Chris. 'Make yourself at home. You can copy your timetable from Gary.'

'Thanks,' said Joe, edging between the tightly packed tables. He nodded to Gary and Chris, and took a neat blue file out of his bag, followed by a ruler and a pencil-case.

'Can I have a look at that timetable then?'

Gary rifled through a folder and finally produced a tattered piece of paper.

'Can you read it?' he said. 'It's a bit of a mess.'

For a moment or two, Chris watched Joe working. He was taking a lot of trouble over a timetable. A total waste of time. Chris had lost his on the first day of term. He always asked Gary if he forgot where he was supposed to be. He got his maths book out. It looked OK, what he'd done; a bit messy, but Chris's work was always messy. He looked at Miss Jones. It was she who'd written the letter to Mum. She didn't look that mean. He could have done without it. Life was complicated enough already. Chris found himself thinking about the night before.

He had been waiting for the phone to ring, and he'd crept out onto the landing to listen.

'You're what?' said Mum's voice. There was a long silence. 'But what about the kids? . . . You hardly see Sarah as it is . . . Once a month! . . . Pull the other one, Colin . . . It'll be once every six months if they're lucky, and you know it . . . You might have come round and told them properly . . . Oh, and you think that'll make everything OK, do you? . . .' Chris decided he'd heard enough, and went back in his room.

Mum had told them at breakfast that Dad was moving to London.

'What difference will that make?' said Sarah. 'He never wants to see me anyway. He just sends me stupid presents that I don't want. He thinks I'm still a kid, Mum.'

'So you don't want him to take you to Alton Towers on Saturday?' said Mum.

Sarah looked up. 'Really? Can I take a friend? I'll ring Hannah.' Sarah was out of the room in a flash, talking on the phone.

'What about you, Chris?' said Mum. 'Why don't you ask Gary to go with you?'

'I don't want to go,' said Chris.

'But why?'

'I just don't, all right?'

'Chris!'

Chris grabbed his bag and left.

In the classroom, Miss Jones was saying something about football.

'. . . so, Under-12's will be on Thursday nights, straight after school. You'll need to see Mr Shepherd and tell him if you're going.'

'What's she on about?' whispered Chris.

'Training,' said Gary. 'Thursday nights for us. You've got to admit, we need it. We could easily have lost last night. What about you, Joe. D'you want to come to football training?'

'No point,' said Joe. 'I'm useless.' He grinned. Being useless didn't seem to bother him.

'Yeah, but it's training,' said Chris. 'You might get better.'

'No chance. I know what I'm talking about. They're my legs.'

'Don't you like football, then?' asked Chris.

'I never said that, did I? Look, I'll tell you what, I'll come to training, and then you'll see. You'll have a laugh, anyway.'

'Great,' said Gary. 'I bet there's people worse than you. Now Kevin's injured we've hardly got enough decent players for a team.' The purple and orange scarf was lying on top of Joe's bag. Gary picked it up as if it was a poisonous snake. 'What *is* this?' he said, 'Tell me it's not a Matfield Town scarf.'

'What if it is?' said Joe.

'It's sad, that's what,' said Gary. 'My grandad used to support them years ago, when they were in the Third Division. Even he wouldn't wear a thing like that now.'

'Don't you read the papers?' said Joe. 'Matfield are going places.'

'You're crazy,' said Chris. Matfield Town had about fifty supporters and they played in the Dudley Morgan Tyres League.

'You wait and see. They're in the second round of the FA Cup.' Joe hesitated, then added, 'My dad's helping with the coaching.'

'Oh, yeah?' said Gary, laughing. 'Very funny.'

Chris looked at Joe, not sure if he believed

24

him. Joe looked like he didn't care whether they believed him or not.

'You'll see,' he said. He stood up. 'Are we going to sit here all morning, or are you going to show me where we go for maths?' Joe handed Gary his timetable and slipped his own copy into a new plastic wallet.

'What do you think?' said Gary to Chris at break.

'About what?' Chris was wondering what Mum would say about the football training.

'About the new kid. Joe. Is he weird, or what?'

'He seemed OK to me,' said Chris. 'It's a pity he's no good at football, though.'

CHAPTER 3

'Training!' said Mum that night, when Chris told her. 'Give me one good reason why I should let you go.'

'I've got to, Mum. If I don't he'll leave me out. This new bloke's not like Mr Reddy. He's serious. You should have seen him last night. And I don't think he likes me either. I've got to be there, Mum.'

There was a silence.

'I'll do a deal with you,' said Mum. 'You get your room tidy, and I mean really tidy – then you can go to football training. Oh, and don't think I've forgotten about the homework, because I haven't. I'm going to ring Miss Jones on Friday night to see how things are going.'

'I can't tidy my room *and* do my homework.'

'I'm sure your friends manage,' said Mum. 'Sarah doesn't have a problem. I can walk across her floor without breaking my neck.'

'You don't have to go in my room.'

'Oh, I do,' Mum told him. 'But I'm not arguing about it. That's the deal. Take it or leave it.'

Chris tidied his room. It didn't take as long as he had expected. He was wondering how he was going to sneak five mouldy coffee cups downstairs when Mum poked her head round the door.

'Thanks.' She reached for the cups and looked around. 'I'm impressed. It's not all under the bed, is it?'

Chris lifted the edge of the bedspread to show her.

'Great,' said Mum. 'Now, I'd like you and Sarah to go across the road and invite the new people over for a cup of tea. They've been moving in all day and I expect they'd like to get away from the chaos.'

'But . . .'

'It's either that or you wash these and I'll nip across the road.'

'OK,' said Chris. 'You win.'

The removal van had been there that

morning, but Chris hadn't paid it much attention. He had lived in Raidon Street all his life. The houses were terraced, but they were big. Tall and narrow. Long front gardens protected them from the busy street. Old people lived in most of the houses. The garden of No 31 was full of flowerpots. Most of them seemed to contain dead plants. Chris walked up the path and knocked on the door.

'Hi.' Chris recognized the man at once. Joe's dad. Chris looked past him into a hallway stacked high with boxes. A bare lightbulb swung from a wire.

'We live across the street,' said Chris. 'Mum says would you like a cup of tea?'

'Katy!' The man yelled up the stairs. 'Our new neighbours are here. They want to know if we want a cup of tea.' A figure in orange overalls appeared. Her face was streaked with dirt.

'I'd love one,' she said. 'But I'll have to get cleaned up first. Where's Joe?'

'Out in the back garden, digging,' said Joe's dad. 'Give us five minutes, and we'll be over.'

'I'm Ian Rawson,' Joe's dad said, when Mum opened the door, 'and this is Katy . . . and Joe.'

'Come on in,' said Mum. 'You must be exhausted. All that stuff to sort out. The kettle's just boiled. Why don't you take Joe next door?' she said to Chris. 'You can watch TV.'

Chris flicked through the channels. There was a match on. UEFA Cup.

'No way,' said Sarah. 'We can watch a video.'

'Oh, go on,' said Joe. 'This Turkish team have got a brilliant central defender. I'd like to see him. Rainford United want to sign him, apparently.'

'You sound like one of those people they have after the match,' said Sarah.

'There he is,' said Joe. 'Selim Volkan.'

On the screen, a tall defender with flowing black hair rose majestically to head a ball clear.

'Oh,' said Sarah, lying down on the carpet near the TV. 'Wow! He's dishy.'

Joe gave Chris a thumbs-up sign. Chris was impressed. They settled down to watch the game.

'This Turkish lot are going to lose,' said Joe, after they had been watching for ten minutes. 'They're pushing both full-backs in advance of the central defenders. It's very naive. Against Inter Roma! They're asking for trouble.'

'Selim will save them,' muttered Sarah, dreamily.

It all looked pretty boring to Chris. There hadn't been one shot on goal.

'It's like chess,' said Joe. 'There! Look at that!'

An Inter midfielder spun on the ball and played a perfect pass into the path of Chester Smith, Inter's young English striker. Smith ran on and scored. The Turkish defenders ran to the referee, screaming for offside. The ref shook his head and pointed to the centre.

'See,' said Joe, as they watched the replay. 'Look at the space behind the full-back. Smith runs wide. The central defenders play him on-side, and then he's just too fast for them.'

'You sound like a book,' said Chris. 'How come you know so much?'

'Dad was a footballer,' said Joe.

'What do you mean, was?'

'He got injured,' said Joe. 'He had to give up. If you think I'm an expert, you should hear Dad.'

'And he's really coaching Matfield Town? You weren't making it up?'

'Their manager used to play with him. Dad's been staying over here in bed-and-breakfast. He started a new job a few months ago, but we couldn't find a house. You should have heard Mum when she found out what Dad had been doing. She went crazy. She's always on at him to forget about football. There's not much chance of that though.'

Sarah groaned as another Inter goal went in. Selim Volkan had missed a header and now he was banging his head on the ground.

'Poor bloke,' said Sarah. 'He did his best.'

'It was very quiet in there,' said Mum, when the new neighbours had gone.

'We watched a football match,' said Chris.

'What, Sarah too? I don't believe it.'

Sarah was still sitting in front of the TV. She had taped the second half. Now she was running a sequence of Selim Volkan making a slow-motion tackle over and over again.

'She's in love,' said Chris.

'Well,' said Mum. 'They seemed very nice. It's good to have some other kids in the street at last. And now you'd better go and do that homework.'

Chris went upstairs and looked for his homework diary. He knew where he'd chucked it. On top of the football magazines. Only he'd tidied them up. He'd put them in boxes on top of the cupboard. He couldn't face getting them all out again. There was always Gary. Chris switched the computer on.

'Not again,' said Gary next day, when Chris asked him if he could look at his homework. 'Why can't you do your own for a change?'

'I would have done. Only I had to tidy my room. And then . . . Go on, Gary, let's have a look.'

'Do it tonight,' said Gary. 'It doesn't have to be in till tomorrow.'

Chris stared at him.

'I don't see why I should get in trouble because of you, that's all. What do I get out of it? You don't even pass to me.'

'Not that again.' Chris was getting angry. 'You said they were brilliant goals.'

'Yeah, well, maybe I've been thinking about things. So do your own homework, all right?'

Mr Shepherd was waiting for them on the field after school.

'OK,' he said. 'We'll get warmed up straight away.' There were one or two groans. 'Nobody kicks a ball around here without warming up,' he continued. 'You do things my way or you go home. Let's get on with it.'

After the warm-ups, he took them for a run round the field. As soon as Chris saw Joe running, he could see why Joe said he was useless. It wasn't Joe's fault. His legs were thin and bony. They didn't look like a footballer's legs at all. Joe laughed.

'See,' he said. 'What did I tell you?'

It was a long way round the field, and as they finished the first circuit Chris felt a stitch beginning in his side. He couldn't believe it when he saw Mr Shepherd setting out on a second lap. He could see the others wincing. Pete Johnson was struggling to keep up, but Gary was jogging along easily. Chris gritted his teeth and forced himself on. The pain in his side was a little easier, but now his legs were starting to feel heavy. He dropped back through the straggling line of runners, and there was nothing he could do about it. He found himself running beside Joe. Joe was smiling to himself as he plodded along.

'I can't go fast,' he said, 'but I can keep going. Are you OK?'

Chris had no breath for talking. He nodded, grimaced, and forced himself on. When he finished he fell to his knees, gasping air into his lungs.

'Don't sit around,' said Mr Shepherd. 'I

don't want you getting cold. Find a partner and grab a ball. Simple pass and control first. You. Gary, is it . . . ? We'll show them.'

As Mr Shepherd demonstrated the exercise with Gary, Chris fought to recover. By the time he stood up, everyone had a partner and they'd all started working.

'Right then, Chris,' said Mr Shepherd, 'you'd better work with me to start with. Let's see what you can do.'

Mr Shepherd chucked the ball at him.

'That's it. Great control. Now chip it back.'

The teacher threw the ball at him again, higher this time. Chris took it on his chest and dropped it neatly to the ground with one touch. Then he chipped it back again. Instantly the ball came back at him, and again, and again. Mr Shepherd didn't let up for a moment. Sometimes it came high, sometimes low. Sometimes it came incredibly fast. Chris was OK to start with, but he hadn't really recovered from the run. His legs started to wobble and his stitch came back. He crouched down, breathing hard.

'Terrific,' said Mr Shepherd. 'Why don't you chuck a few to me while you get your breath back?'

Chris stood up slowly. He was sure Mr Shepherd was laughing at him. His temper

34

flared. He reckoned everything the teacher knew about football came out of a book. He picked up the ball and threw it, fast and high. He couldn't believe his eyes. Somehow, Mr Shepherd took all the pace off the ball with his head. The ball dropped gently; and it seemed to fall for a long time before the teacher's foot connected with it and sent it flying back towards him. He was still standing with his mouth open in astonishment when the ball thudded into his stomach. The next moment he found himself sitting in the mud, and he heard the sound of laughter.

CHAPTER 4

Chris tried to catch his breath. There was a small ripple of applause from the kids nearby. Mr Shepherd turned on them.

'You're supposed to be working. Get on with it. Right, Chris, let's have another one.'

After a few minutes, Mr Shepherd moved on. He sent Pete to work with Chris.

'Running and passing across the field and back,' said Mr Shepherd. 'Keep the passes short and fast. Off you go.'

'Come on,' said Pete. 'What's up with you?' Chris wasn't sure his legs would carry him across the field. Pete hit the ball to him. He controlled it and passed it back into Pete's path.

'First time you've passed to anyone this

year,' said Pete, stabbing the ball back towards Chris.

'You what?' Chris stopped running. The ball flashed past him, but he ignored it.

'You heard,' Pete replied. 'Everyone says so.'

'Yeah, and what about you?' demanded Chris, flushing.

'You two,' yelled Mr Shepherd. 'Get on with it!'

Chris turned and walked off after the ball.

'Watch it!' yelled Gary.

Chris paused. Gary was racing across the field, trading passes with Phil Grant. It looked like a different Gary to the one Chris knew. Or maybe Gary had changed, and Chris hadn't noticed before. Gary was good. Suddenly, Gary looked like a real footballer.

'Put those balls away,' said Mr Shepherd. 'We'll play some five-a-sides now. Get a move on, Chris.'

'He *has* got it in for me,' thought Chris. He forced himself into a jog. 'He'll probably make me go in goal.'

Chris was wrong. By the time he returned to the group, Mr Shepherd had nearly finished sorting out the teams.

'OK, Chris. I've put you with the blues. You can play up front. That's where you normally play, right? You're playing against the reds on that pitch there.'

Gary and Phil were both on the red team. There was a new kid in the reds as well, Andy Maxwell. Chris hadn't seen him play before. Chris's team had Jez in goal, then there were Ranjiv and Pete. 'Joe, you can go with the blues, too,' said Mr Shepherd.

'Tough luck on you,' said Joe to Chris. 'I'll stay out of the way on the wing, OK? Just don't ask me to do any running.'

'You know what I want to see,' said Mr Shepherd. 'I want to see you working for each other. I want to see you thinking. I want to see you passing the ball. Now get on with it.'

Chris touched the ball to Pete. Pete turned and played it back towards his mate, Ranjiv. The pass wasn't strong enough, and Phil nipped forward and cut it out easily. He gave the ball to Gary, and Gary slid it on to Andy. Joe was doing his best, chasing around, but he simply wasn't quick enough. Ranjiv and Pete were desperate. Chris hovered on the halfway line as usual.

'Mark him, Chris!' Pete screamed, pointing at Phil Grant. 'Mark *someone*!'

It was too late. Phil received another

pin-point pass from Gary and he gave Jez no chance with the shot.

'Why didn't you get back?' said Pete. 'They're not even bothering to mark you. There's four of them on to three of us.'

'Oh, come on,' said Chris. 'All you've got to do is get a tackle in and boot it up the field. Then I'll do the business.'

Chris kicked off.

'Go on then,' said Pete. He booted the ball forward into space. Chris sprinted after it. He kept it in play by the touchline. Phil came to him instantly. Chris stepped over the ball, feinted to go right, and pushed the ball between Phil's legs. A perfect nutmeg!

Chris was away. The ball was at his feet and everything was fine. Then suddenly there was a flash of red at his shoulder. It was Gary. Chris was so surprised he took his eye off the ball. It rolled harmlessly into the area. The keeper picked it up and threw it out, straight to Gary.

Gary ran, with the ball at his feet. He raced past Joe, and then past Pete. Ranjiv backed away from him, not sure what to do. Gary was going like a train. He ran the length of the pitch and there was never any doubt that he was going to score.

'Why didn't you tackle him?' said Chris. 'Why'd you back off like that?'

'You think you're so good, why don't you have a go?' said Ranjiv.

'I'd be better than you, anyway,' said Chris.

'Yeah? Well show us then. Go on.'

Before Chris could reply, Mr Shepherd arrived.

'What's happening here? Why have you stopped playing?'

'Chris reckons he'd be good in defence,' said Ranjiv.

'That's right,' said Gary. Chris saw him grin at Ranjiv. 'And we need defenders, don't we, sir?'

'Great idea, Chris,' said Mr Shepherd. 'We'll give it a try.'

'But I didn't say that . . .'

'Just get on with it, lads. We'll see how it goes.'

Chris glanced over his shoulder as he walked back into the heart of the defence. 'This is stupid,' he muttered to Jez, as he placed himself on the edge of the area. 'It's a waste of time.' Chris was furious with Gary. He could see what Gary was trying to do. It was obvious. Gary wanted to be the striker.

The game restarted. Gary won the ball

right away, and the reds attacked. Chris felt panic hit him. He didn't have a clue what to do. Then he heard Mr Shepherd's voice.

'Mark up, blues! Take a man, Chris. Stay with him.'

Chris looked around. Andy was unmarked. Chris moved up close to him. Phil had the ball out wide. Andy turned and started a run towards the goal. Chris turned to run with him, but even as he turned, something told him that the ball wasn't heading for the same place as Andy was. He veered to his right and launched himself into the air. His header ballooned clear into the other half of the field.

'Great header!' yelled Joe. 'Brilliant, Chris.'

The reds had committed everyone forward in attack. Pete latched on to Chris's header and stuck the ball in the back of the net.

'That should have been me,' thought Chris, as Ranjiv ran over to congratulate Pete. Neither of them mentioned the brilliant header.

The reds attacked again from the kick-off. Two passes and there was Gary, running straight at Chris.

'He's going right,' thought Chris; then, a split second later, 'He's going left.' He found himself backing away, just like the others had done, trying to put off making a decision.

'I've got to go for it,' he told himself. 'NOW!'

He lunged forward, eye on the ball, but Gary seemed to change gear and Chris's boot connected with empty space. He didn't have to turn round to know that Gary had scored. He hit the ground in frustration. Who'd want to be a defender? He looked over to the touchline.

'You're doing OK,' said Mr Shepherd. 'Gary was too good, that's all.'

Gary bent to give him a hand up. Chris ignored him.

'Tough luck, mate,' said Gary. 'Just not quick enough!' Then he was gone, leaving Chris bursting with anger.

'Next time,' he told himself. 'Next time I'll have him.'

Anger made Chris concentrate. He pounced on every loose ball. He stayed back, holding his position, watching for Gary to make a move. He didn't have long to wait. Gary had the ball in the centre circle. He turned fast, beat one player, and moved quickly towards Chris. There was a yell from the wing. It was Joe.

'Stay on your feet, Chris. Watch the ball!'

Chris didn't need telling. Gary swayed to

the left, but Chris kept his eyes firmly on the ball at Gary's feet. Gary flicked it with the outside of his right foot, and Chris was on it in a flash. Gary went flying past, but Chris had the ball!

Ahead of him, on the halfway line, he could see the blue tops of Ranjiv and Pete. There was only one red defender. Chris leant back and hit a pass over the defender's head into the empty spaces of the other half. Ranjiv ran on and scored. Gary climbed to his feet, shaking his head.

'I never thought you could do it,' he said.

'Well, I have,' said Chris, 'and now I've had enough. Who wants to watch other people score all the goals?' A few minutes later Mr Shepherd called them together.

'You've all worked hard,' he said. 'I know it's not easy, changing the way you play. Next week we've got the semi-final of the Cup. If you remember the things we've been working on today, I reckon you've a good chance of winning. Now then, Gary. How would you feel about playing up front? Right up front?'

'Great,' said Gary. 'I mean, thanks.'

'Good,' said Mr Shepherd, 'because that frees Chris to play in the centre of the defence. Maybe that'll stop us leaking so many goals. You played a blinder, Chris. Well done.'

Chris felt numb. He didn't hear the rest of the team. HE was the striker. Gary was good, OK, but being striker was Chris's job. There was no way he was going to be a defender. Blood rushed to his head. It had been a bad couple of days, and now Mr Shepherd was trying to make him look stupid. Well they could manage without him then. He started walking towards the changing rooms.

'Chris?' said Mr Shepherd. 'We haven't finished. You need to warm down. We don't want you getting injured before the game.'

'Stuff the stupid game,' said Chris. 'And the warm-downs. And the warm-ups, too. I'm not a defender. I don't want to be a defender. If I can't be a striker, I don't want to play.'

There were tears in his eyes as he walked back across the field.

CHAPTER 5

Chris walked into the changing room and kicked the wall. He sat on the bench for a moment with his head in his hands as the shouts echoed out on the field. It was Gary's fault. He remembered Gary grinning at Ranjiv out on the pitch. Gary had changed. Then, suddenly, he could hear Gary's voice in his head: '*Why don't you do your own homework?*' He'd forgotten about the homework. There was no way he'd be able to do it himself. He couldn't even remember what it was – something for science. He'd get done, and everything would just go on getting worse. He looked over to Gary's bag, hanging on its peg. Why not? If he was quick he could copy it out of Gary's book before they came in. Gary owed him.

The bag was hanging above Gary's neatly piled clothes. Chris jumped on a bench and looked through the wired glass of the window. It had started to rain, but they were all still doing some stupid routine on the field. He could hear the distant sound of Mr Shepherd's voice. He took the bag off the peg and pulled out Gary's science book.

The homework was just a load of formulas. Everyone's would be the same anyway. Chris stood on the bench, balancing Gary's book on the window ledge, and started to write quickly. As he finished the last line, he looked up and saw the others walking across the playground. In a few seconds they'd be coming through the door of the changing room. Chris jumped down from the bench and stuffed Gary's book back in his bag. There wasn't time to put the bag on the peg. Chris sat down with his own book in his hand. His heart was racing. Gary was first through the door.

'You idiot. What did you do that for?'

'Do what?' For a moment, Chris thought Gary had seen him with the bag.

'Saying all that to Mr Shepherd. Walking off. You're going to get done, Chris.'

'I'm a striker. I'm not playing in defence.'

'Look, I'm sorry he's made me striker, OK? But we need defenders. You know we do. And you were good. That header . . .'

'You don't have to pretend, Gary. You love it. Gary Roberts, striker. So don't give me that stuff about me being a great defender. It makes me sick.'

'You think everyone's like you, don't you? Some people are just glad they're in the team. You don't care about the team, do you? If you did you wouldn't care what position you played. All you care about is Chris Jackson.'

'That's right,' said Pete. 'I'm in midfield. I'd rather be up front.'

'Don't make me laugh,' said Chris. He was almost shouting, and there was no thought in the words he was saying. He felt bad. He just wanted to lash out and hurt someone. 'You can't be in defence because you can't tackle, and you can't be up front because you can't shoot. You're useless.'

'That's not true,' said Ranjiv angrily. He was holding Pete back. 'We all know what's wrong with this team.'

'Oh, yeah?' sneered Chris. 'Why don't you tell us then?'

The room fell silent. 'OK, then,' said

Ranjiv. 'You asked for it. It's *you*. You run around on the halfway line waiting for everyone else to do the work. You never get back and help. That's why we let so many goals in.' The others were nodding. Chris looked at Gary, but Gary wouldn't meet his eyes. Slowly, the others started to change. Chris shivered. He felt cold inside for a second. Then anger took over again. It was all lies. I don't care what they think, he told himself. He dressed quickly, then elbowed his way through the sweaty crowd and into the empty corridor. Only the corridor wasn't empty. Mr Shepherd was waiting for him.

'Well?' he said. 'What have you got to say for yourself?'

Chris said nothing.

'Look, Chris, obviously you're upset. But I really think you've got the makings of a great defender. Just think about the difference you made to the blues when you went back in defence. The others could see it, even if you couldn't.'

'Oh, yeah?' said Chris.

'It's what every great team needs. Some-one at the heart of the defence who can read the game . . .' He's nuts, thought Chris. Mr Shepherd was still talking. 'They need you,

Chris. I'm offering you a chance here. I'm willing to pass over the way you behaved out there, and . . .'

Chris laughed bitterly. Mr Shepherd obviously had no idea. Ranjiv's words were still ringing in his ears. 'Forget it,' he said. 'What's the point?'

Mr Shepherd's face changed. 'Fine. If that's the way you want it. But I'm warning you now. Don't think you can change your mind tomorrow and just walk back into the team.'

Mr Shepherd turned to go into the changing room. As he did so, Chris heard Dad's voice. What was he doing here?

'Hey! You! I want to talk to you.' Dad seemed to take for ever to walk along the corridor. It was like a scene out of a nightmare. When he arrived he was out of breath. 'What's going on? Why was Chris playing in defence? He's a striker.'

'I take it you're Mr Jackson.' Mr Shepherd held out a hand. Dad ignored it.

'That's right.'

'Well, perhaps you could talk some sense into your son. He's a good player, but he's got a lot to learn. Right now, the team needs defenders. I gave Chris a chance and he turned it down. It's as simple as that. Now, if you

49

don't mind, I've got children to supervise.'

Mr Shepherd went to open the door. Chris's dad moved quickly in front of him.

'What do you mean, he turned it down? Turned what down? What's he on about, Chris?'

'Just leave it, Dad,' said Chris. 'Please.'

'I should take your son's advice, Mr Jackson. Let him tell you what happened, then make an appointment to see me, if that's what you want.' The swing doors crashed shut behind Mr Shepherd.

'Well?' said Dad. 'I was watching from the road. It was pure luck I was passing. You should have told me you had training.'

'I don't need this, Dad. I don't need you. I can sort it out myself.'

'You're not making a very good job of it, are you?'

'He wanted me to play in defence. That's all. And I said no. Satisfied?'

Chris turned and started walking quickly down the corridor.

'Chris, wait!' Dad hurried after him. 'I'm just trying to help. The guy's an idiot.'

Chris walked on in silence. They were through the gates now, walking along the street. They came to Dad's car. Chris kept going.

'Come on, Chris. Get in. This is ridiculous.'

Chris stopped. 'I don't want your help,' he said. 'Not that kind of help. You made me look stupid. I don't know why you even bothered. Even if I was in the team, you wouldn't be here to see me play, would you?'

'That's not fair. I told you, it's the job.'

'And her,' said Chris. He turned, and carried on walking.

Dad grabbed his shoulder, spinning him round. He was angry, upset. 'You haven't even met Mandy,' he said. 'You know nothing about her.'

'No,' said Chris. 'Can I go now, please?' There was a pause, then Dad took his hand from Chris's shoulder.

'I'll see you Saturday, then,' Dad said, finally. 'Alton Towers.'

'I'm not coming. I wouldn't come if you paid me.'

Chris walked away quickly. When he reached the corner, he looked back. Dad was still standing by the car, staring after him.

Chris was turning into Raidon Street when he heard the footsteps behind him.

'Chris!' He turned and saw Joe, jogging steadily along the pavement.

'What do you want?'

'Nothing.'

'You were running after me,' Chris accused him.

'I like running. I run everywhere. It's not a crime, is it? I thought you might want to come round mine.'

'Why would I want to do that?' As soon as he said the words, Chris wished he could call them back.

'OK.' Joe held one hand up, as if to deflect Chris's anger. 'All I was going to say was, I thought you looked good when you were in defence. Really good. I reckon that . . .'

'Just shut up, OK?' Chris was shouting. 'It's nothing to do with you. Nothing. It's nothing to do with anyone. I'm going home.'

'Don't!' said Mum, as Chris opened the door.

'I haven't even come in yet,' said Chris. 'Don't what?'

'Don't chuck that bag on the floor by the washing-machine. If you do, I promise you, I'll scream.'

Chris stopped himself in mid-throw.

'Put the bag down,' said Mum. 'Take out the stinking mess inside, and put it in the machine.' Sarah was sitting at the kitchen table, laughing at him. Chris was too shocked to argue. He bundled the football kit into the washing-machine.

'OK,' said Mum. 'That wasn't too hard was it? Now put some powder in. Great. And switch it on. Terrific. That little job just cost you sixty seconds of your life.'

'It's a blitz,' said Sarah. 'It's not just you. There's a list. Look.'

A piece of paper was pinned to a cupboard door. There were three names at the top. *Mum*, *Sarah* and *Chris*. Under each name there was a list of jobs. Mum's list was three times as long as the other two. At the bottom of the list was: GO TO WORK. That bit was written in red.

'You've got a job,' said Chris.

'I start on Monday. And if you two don't help out it'll probably kill me.'

Mum had been at college for almost as long as Chris could remember; since before Dad left anyway. She'd finished last year, and she'd been trying for a job ever since. She'd been to hundreds of interviews and got nothing.

'You didn't say. I mean, I didn't realize you had an interview,' said Chris, looking doubtfully at his list of jobs.

'Yes, well, with everything that happened

last night I forgot to mention it. You might look pleased.'

'I . . . I am,' said Chris. 'Of course I am.'

'We're having a little celebration,' said Mum. Chris looked at the table. There was a bottle of wine, and Coke, and nibbles, and the best plates.

'I invited our new neighbours round,' Mum continued. 'They're bringing some pizzas. You've got about half an hour to get your homework done. How did the training go?'

It was the first time Mum had ever asked about football. Chris couldn't remember when he'd last seen her looking this happy. He didn't know what to say.

'Chris? What's wrong? You're as white as a sheet.'

Chris sat down at the table. Mum put her hand on his forehead. Chris brushed it away.

'I'm OK, Mum. Just a bit tired, that's all.'

'You sit there. I'll get you a cup of tea.'

'I told you, I'm OK. I'm going to my room.'

Chris closed his bedroom door and they were all staring at him. The strikers. Shearer, Cole, Wright, Zola, Ronaldo, Mueller. Not a defender in sight. Defenders were the enemy. Defenders were boring. How had everything gone so wrong?

CHAPTER 6

Ian Rawson arrived late. The bell rang as Mum was cutting up the pizzas.

'I didn't change,' he said. 'I came straight round when I found the note.' He was wearing a tracksuit.

'What took you so long?' asked Joe's mum, Katy. 'You said you were just popping round for a chat.'

'We started talking about the team. For Saturday. You know what it's like, love.'

'What team's that, then?' said Mum.

'Matfield Town,' said Katy grimly. 'I might have known there was nowhere we could go where he wouldn't find some lame duck football team to help. He just can't keep away. He's like a big kid.'

'Oh, come on, love. Matfield Town aren't lame ducks. This is the second round of the FA Cup. And I couldn't let Alex down. He's an old mate. It's only a bit of coaching.'

'That's what he always says,' Katy told Mum. 'Every town we go to he finds some old mate from his playing days. Ends up spending every evening kicking a ball around and getting covered in mud. Oh, look, I'm sorry – this is supposed to be your celebration. Where's that fizz?'

Chris found it hard to be cheerful. He was pleased for Mum. Really pleased. But he felt like he was at the bottom of a hole and he couldn't see a way out.

'Tell me about Selim Volkan,' Sarah was asking Joe. 'I want to know all about him.'

'It's all in the papers today,' said Joe. 'He's just signed for Rainford United. And there's an article in *Football Fever*. I'll bring it over.'

'Chris gets *Football Fever*,' said Sarah. 'Chris? Have you got that one?'

'Perhaps,' said Chris.

'Go on, have a look. Please.'

Chris found the magazine. Joe was drooling over his computer.

'You mean this is all yours? You don't have to share it?'

Chris nodded. 'It was for me and Sarah,

really. Last Christmas. But Sarah won't even look at it.'

'Unbelievable. What games have you got? Wow! *Rally Magic*. Can I have a go?'

'Sure,' said Chris. 'Help yourself.'

Joe was brilliant at computer games. His best time round the Welsh mountains was twenty-three minutes better than Chris's. Chris watched him steer through an iced-up river at fifty miles an hour.

'You know what?' said Joe, without taking his eyes off the screen.

'What?'

'You could be a pretty good defender. If you wanted.'

For a second, Chris's temper flared again. Then he felt guilty. None of this was Joe's fault. He was surprised Joe was still talking to him after the way he'd been earlier.

'Well I don't want to, OK?' said Chris. 'I'm a striker. And if I can't be a striker I'm not interested.'

'You can't tell me you didn't get a buzz out of stopping Gary. It was a brilliant tackle. Total destruction.'

'It's not like scoring though. Nothing like it.'

'Depends whether you like knocking things down, or building them. Me, I love

57

seeing those big steel balls smashing into old buildings. Defenders are destroyers.' Joe smashed his car through a row of straw bales and headed for the finish. 'There. Forty-seven minutes. Beat that.'

Chris couldn't sleep that night. He woke up with Joe's voice running round in his head. *You could be a pretty good defender* . . . All kinds of stupid questions kept popping into his mind. What if I am a defender? I stopped Gary, didn't I? Maybe it's true. He found himself thinking about the way the game had looked from the centre of the defence. Being there was like being in the driver's seat, right in the middle of things. That's all rubbish, said another part of him. Just because it's interesting, that doesn't mean *I* have to do it. Someone else can do it if they think it's so important. Wait and see how many goals they score with Gary up front instead of me.

'OK,' said Mr Sutton, the science teacher. 'Homework. We have a mystery. Perhaps some of you can solve it for me. Here we have Gary Roberts's homework. And here we have Chris Jackson's homework.'
    Chris felt sick.

'Most people, you see,' went on Mr Sutton, 'have transcribed the three results that we discussed in class. Not very original, but predictable. Somehow or other you two have managed to come up with a further seven possible outcomes. And they are identical. I'm simply curious as to how this came about.'

Why didn't he just say it? thought Chris. Everyone knew what he meant. He probably thought he was being funny. One or two kids were sniggering already. He caught Gary's eye by accident and looked away quickly. Why did Gary have to be clever and do three times as much as anyone else?

'We did it together, sir,' said Gary. 'That's OK isn't it? I thought you said it was OK to work together. We talked about it and then we wrote it down.'

Mr Sutton was stopped in his tracks.

'That's not what I said. But if you say it was a genuine mistake, Gary . . . ?'

'It was, sir. Sorry.'

They were picking teams on the playground at break. Gary and Ranjiv were the captains. No-one spoke to Chris. They just didn't pick him.

Chris put himself on Ranjiv's team.

'Shove off, Chris,' said Ranjiv. 'You're not playing.'

'I can do what I want.'

'Grow up, Chris. Your daddy can't help you here.'

'Leave him, Ranjiv,' said Gary. Ranjiv went back to the game. 'I saw you with my book, you know,' Gary continued. 'It's always been the same, hasn't it – me doing things for you? I'm sick of it. And don't waste your time trying to get back in the team. They're all sick of you, never passing to anyone. Going on about how good you are.'

'Never passing to *you*, that's what you mean. No-one passes. If it hadn't been for me scoring goals we'd never have won a game. You think you can score as many goals as me? Fine. Go ahead and try.'

'You think you're really something, don't you, Chris? You wait and see. The only thing we'll miss will be your stupid celebrations.'

Chris hurled himself at Gary and dragged him to the ground. Gary fought back and landed a punch on Chris's cheek. They rolled over and over on the playground. Chris heard someone yelling at them to stop. Then he felt a hand yank at his shoulder.

'Leave it,' said Joe. Somehow he got

between them, and collected a fist in the stomach for his trouble.

'Watch out,' he gasped.

Chris and Gary stepped back, panting. Then Gary turned and walked away.

'Don't expect me to thank you,' said Chris. His left eye was throbbing.

'I can't see why you were fighting. Gary got you out of trouble, didn't he?'

'Yeah, well he's not going to grass, is he? But he's nicked my place in the team. And he's turned them all against me. I hate him.'

'That's not the way it looks to me. You walked out, didn't you?'

'And so what if I did? They're all rubbish. I wouldn't play for them if you paid me.'

'You don't mean that. Look, if you want any help, my dad . . .'

'I don't want any help,' Chris shouted. 'I don't need any help. Just leave me alone. Stop sticking your nose in. It's nothing to do with you. Not any of it.'

Miss Jones opened the classroom door. 'Whatever it is, save it till after my lesson,' she said. 'Chris; you need to remember I shall be talking to your mother tonight.' She looked at him. 'What have you done to your face? Have you been fighting?'

'I fell over,' said Chris, and he walked past her into the silent classroom.

'I've just been talking to Miss Jones,' said Mum. Chris had been hoping to avoid her. His eye was going to be spectacular. Mum was staring at it now. 'You *have* been fighting, haven't you? Miss Jones said she thought . . .'

'OK, so I had a fight. It happens. It wasn't anyone's fault. I can sort out my own problems.'

'It doesn't look that way to me. Although Miss Jones did say your work's been better. Well, *adequate* was what she said. It's not exactly high praise. She also said there was some problem about football. She said you'd been dropped.'

'That's not true,' said Chris angrily. 'I said I didn't want to play. And I don't. I'd have thought you'd have been pleased about that.' Chris ran up the stairs before Mum could say any more.

The phone rang after tea. Mum answered it. Chris knew it was Dad as soon as he heard Mum's voice change.

'Who else would it be?' she said '. . . I'm not being funny. I know you. You're going to be late, aren't you ? . . . What do you mean, not exactly?'

There was a long silence. It grew longer. Chris and Sarah could hear Dad's voice. Mum put the receiver down without saying another word.

'What did he say?' asked Sarah.

'Don't be stupid,' said Chris. 'He's not coming, is he, Mum? You can kiss goodbye to your Alton Towers trip.'

Sarah burst into tears.

'Sometimes, Chris, I feel like thumping you myself,' said Mum. She put her arm round Sarah. 'Look, we'll do something good tomorrow, all of us. I promise.'

Chris woke up late the next morning. When he went into the kitchen Mum was smiling.

'Well,' she said, 'how about going to a football match today?'

'You don't mean it? You hate football.'

'Well, just this once I'll make an exception. It's all arranged. It was Sarah's idea.'

Sarah was sitting at the kitchen table with a pile of *Football Fever* magazines.

'Hey!' said Chris. 'You nicked them from my room. Tell her to put them back, Mum.'

'It's the legs,' said Sarah, paying no attention to Chris. 'Their legs are just fantastic.'

There was a knock at the door.

'Hi,' said Joe. 'It's all arranged. Dad's well

pleased. You'll be sitting right behind the dugout. Hey, Chris – Dad says you can come and sit on the bench if you want.'

'You mean we're going to watch Matfield Town?' said Chris.

'The greatest day in their history,' said Joe.

Chris replied before he could stop himself. 'Not much of a history, then, is it?' he said. And then he felt terrible. He'd woken with the events of the previous day running through his mind. If Joe hadn't stopped him, the fight with Gary could have been bad. He could have got himself chucked out of school. He hadn't exactly been grateful. He was amazed that Joe had bothered to get the tickets.

'It's the second round of the FA Cup,' said Mum. Suddenly, she was an expert on football. 'If they win this they could be drawn against somebody famous. Anyway, Chris, if you don't want to come, you can always stay at home.'

Mum was angry. Chris knew he'd been mean. And he was curious, too – curious about Joe, and about Joe's dad, and even, he realized, about Matfield Town.

'No, it's OK.' He turned to Joe. 'Look, I'm sorry,' he said. 'Can I really sit on the bench?'

CHAPTER 7

Matfield's ground was in the middle of the industrial estate. They caught a bus most of the way and got off outside the tractor factory. Rows of green tractors gleamed in the autumn sunshine. Chris was amazed to see that there were hundreds of people on their way to the match. And they weren't all old people either.

'It's a sell-out,' said Joe. 'You were lucky. Dad had some tickets, but he didn't know who to give them to.'

'Where's your mum?' asked Sarah. 'Is she there already?'

'She wouldn't come,' said Joe. 'If she had her way, Dad wouldn't even watch football on TV. But she knows she can't stop him. *He* says it's in his blood.'

The people walking along the broken pavement between the factories were laughing and joking. Some of them were wearing Matfield Town scarves. There was no chanting though, not like the crowds Chris had seen on TV. It was more like Saturday afternoon shopping.

The entrance to the ground was sandwiched between a builder's yard and a high brick wall that stretched off into the distance. A couple of harassed-looking men were checking people's tickets on the gate.

'My dad's left some tickets for us,' said Joe.

'Oh, yeah? And who are you?'

'Joe Rawson. Ian Rawson's my dad.'

'Well, I don't know nothing about no tickets, son. Better try in there.'

On the wall of a low brick building, huge plastic letters spelt out ' ATFIELD TOW FC'. Blue paint was peeling off the doors. Inside, the bar had been turned into a makeshift ticket office.

'I've never seen anything like it,' said the large, red-faced woman who handed over the tickets. 'Not in thirty years, I haven't. I'm not sure I could cope if we win.'

'Not much chance of that,' muttered Chris.

He was starting to think it had been a mistake to come, after all.

Mum gave him an angry shove, and they pushed their way out through the crowd.

'It may not mean much to you,' she said, 'but you don't have to be rude.'

'You'll see,' Joe told him. 'They're a lot better than you think.'

They emerged from the office, and the pitch was right in front of them. They were standing near a corner flag. A single white rail ran around three sides of the pitch, to keep the spectators back. On the fourth side was the stand. The roof and the sides were covered with rusting corrugated iron, but the seats were full, and along the front of the stand was a row of brand-new advertising hoardings. Someone had repainted the sign above the stand too, so that the words MATFIELD TOWN FC stood out brightly against the dull red of the rusting iron.

'Where do we go?' said Sarah. 'There's no room in there.'

'Yes there is,' said Joe. 'Come on.'

He led the way along the side of the pitch behind the goal. The goal nets, and even the goal posts themselves looked brand-new. The lines around the edge of the carefully mown grass were sharp-edged and perfect. In the

stand someone began to shout: MATFIELD . . .
MATFIELD . . . MATFIELD . . . People around the
ground took up the chant, and even Chris
couldn't stop himself feeling a little excited,
especially when the far end of the stand
erupted in red and white fans chanting,
HAVERSTONE . . . HAVERSTONE . . . It was
beginning to feel like a real match after all.

Mum and Sarah found their seats in the
stand. Chris and Joe waited by the white
railing behind the dugout as the two teams
ran onto the field.

'But that's our milkman,' said Sarah,
pointing to the tall dark man with the No 9
on his back.

'And that's the builder my friend Jenny's
going out with,' said Mum. 'You remember,
he used to come round, Bob somebody.' Mum
waved and yelled. Bob saw her and grinned
nervously.

Chris was watching the Matfield players
too. This close, you could almost feel the
nerves. They had a right to be worried,
thought Chris. The Haverstone players all
looked enormous. He watched a couple of them
warming up. They're showing off, he thought,
as the Haverstone No 9 juggled the ball a few
times, before back-heeling it to a teammate.
They think they're going to walk it.

'Hi, lads.' Joe's dad was standing beside them. 'This is my old mate Alex. Alex Matthews.' He patted the stocky, balding man beside him on the shoulder. 'Alex, this is Joe, and his friend Chris.'

'Good to meet you lads,' said Alex, shaking their hands. 'It's a great day. A great day. I just wish I didn't feel so . . .'

'Alex is more nervous than the lads,' said Ian, laughing. 'Calm down, Alex, or you'll lose the rest of your hair. I just want a few last words with them. You sit down before your legs give way.'

Alex Matthews sat down on the bench. The ref blew his whistle, and the two captains ran to the centre of the pitch. The substitutes jogged over and sat on the bench behind the boys.

'Shove up then,' said Ian. 'This is it. We're off!'

As he sat down, the top of his tracksuit fell open and Chris caught a glimpse of an orange and purple shirt underneath. Joe saw the same thing.

'Dad,' he said. 'Why are you . . . ?'

But he never finished his question. The match had begun.

Right from the start, Haverstone attacked. From the kick-off the ball came flying out to the Haverstone No 10 who was standing on the touchline right in front of Chris. Chris was so close that he heard him grunt as he controlled the ball on his chest. Then he raced away down the line. He beat two Matfield players easily. Ian was on his feet, hands cupped to his mouth, screaming at the Matfield defence. The No 10 looked up, and crossed the ball into the penalty area. The Matfield goalkeeper started to come out.

'No!' yelled Ian and Alex together.

Bob Dixon jumped to head the ball clear, but the Haverstone striker was already airborne, and the ball crashed into the net to thunderous applause from the Haverstone fans. Chris had to stop himself joining in. It was a brilliant goal, even if it was a defensive error. He wouldn't have minded scoring it himself. But all around him there was a stunned silence.

The Haverstone players were laughing and congratulating each other. You would have thought the game was already over. Their fans were chanting EASY . . . EASY . . . EASY . . .

Ian was on his feet again, gesturing with his hands, trying to calm the Matfield players. Alex Matthews reached up and pulled him back onto the bench.

'Now you know what it's like. You try to drum it into them, but they get out on the pitch and they forget everything you've said. It's no good yelling at them. They can't even hear you.'

Ian sat down, shaking his head. 'If I was out there . . .'

'Don't even think about it,' said Alex, sharply.

Minutes passed and Haverstone didn't score again. The Matfield players began to settle to their game. They worked hard, making one tackle after another. Wave after wave of Haverstone attacks came to nothing. After twenty minutes the Matfield keeper pulled off a terrific save from a volley that looked completely unstoppable. The crowd began to make a surprising amount of noise, and Chris found himself yelling too. He could hear Mum and Sarah shouting in the stand behind him.

'Come on, Matfield!' yelled Mum. 'You can do it!'

Ian turned to the boys. 'The nerves have gone now,' he said. 'They're starting to play some football at last.'

Matfield were defending well. Everyone on the team was chasing back, harrying the Haverstone players, never letting them settle on the ball. In the centre of the defence, Bob Dixon seemed to have got the measure of the Haverstone striker. He was winning everything in the air now, but still Matfield couldn't get out of their own half, and Stan Darrowby, their striker, had hardly touched the ball.

Chris saw the ref look at his watch. The first half was nearly over and still Haverstone pressed forward. The Haverstone winger finally realized that high crosses were a waste of time, and he hit a low ball in to the feet of the No 9. Bob Dixon saw it coming. He stepped forward quickly and intercepted the pass. It was almost the first time in the game he had had the ball at his feet. Chris saw him look up. Stan Darrowby turned suddenly away from the defender beside him, and raced towards the halfway line. Bob Dixon hit the pass, curving sweetly into Stan's path, piercing the Haverstone defence.

Chris leapt up, yelling at the top of his voice. Stan Darrowby was clear. The Haverstone defenders were fast, but they couldn't catch Stan. With the crowd roaring him on he took the ball round the keeper and rolled it into the empty net. As the crowd and the players celebrated, the ref blew the whistle for half-time.

Chris and Joe joined Mum and Sarah.

'Well?' said Mum, as they munched hot-dogs. 'Are you glad you came?'

'It's great,' said Chris. 'But they'll never win. Haverstone won't make another mistake like that.'

'Of course they'll win,' said Mum. 'They've got to.'

'You're not actually enjoying a football match, are you, Mum?' asked Chris.

'I don't know what's happened to me,' said Mum. 'I haven't got a clue what they're all shouting about, but I know I don't want those Haverstone people to win.'

'Well, I think we can do it,' said Joe. 'If Bob Dixon keeps playing like that, they'll never get past him.'

The second half started very differently from the first.

'What's going on?' said Chris. 'Something's changed.'

Matfield pressed forward. It seemed as if they had an extra man on the field. There was always someone for the player on the ball to pass to.

'Another man in midfield,' said Joe. 'Dad's decided Bob Dixon can handle their striker on his own. That's it, isn't it, Dad?'

'You'd better pray that I'm right,' said Ian Rawson.

For a few crucial minutes, Haverstone failed to cope with the extra man. The crowd began to sense that the impossible might happen. There was a roar as Stan Darrowby picked up the ball and made a darting run on the edge of the area. A desperate challenge came in, then another. Stan hit the ground and the whistle blew. The crowd screamed for a penalty, but the referee pointed to a spot just outside the box. Bob Dixon ran forward for the free kick.

'This is it!' said Ian. 'It's perfect.'

'I can't watch,' said Alex. He buried his head in his hands.

'I've watched them practise this,' said Joe.

'Shut up, Joe,' said Ian.

A Matfield player ran over the ball, then another player chipped the ball over the Haverstone wall and Chris saw Bob Dixon rise above a crowd of players. The ball flew into the top corner and the crowd went wild. The substitutes and Alex Matthews and Ian and the trainer were all hugging each other and yelling.

'He's still down,' said Joe.

'What?' said Ian.

'Bob Dixon. He's still down.'

The trainer grabbed his bag and sprinted onto the pitch. The referee was signalling for a stretcher.

'I don't believe it!' said Alex Matthews. 'This can't be happening to me.' He turned to the tallest of the substitutes. 'Come on, Jason, you'd better get warmed up.'

'No!' said Ian. He was stripping off his tracksuit. 'We need experience out there, Alex. You know it and I know it. I'm going on.'

CHAPTER 8

'No way, Ian,' said Alex. 'There's nearly half the match left. Anything could happen.'

'Oh come on, Alex. This is the chance of a lifetime. If we hold on for another forty minutes, we'll be in the third round. If we draw a big club, you could rebuild the whole ground on the proceeds. I always said I'd play in an emergency. That's why I registered.'

'You know this isn't what I meant. Playing five minutes as a sub at the end of a local league game, that's one thing. You're talking about half a match against professionals. You know what could happen.'

'He's right, Dad,' said Joe. 'You can't.'

'I'm going to play, Joe. I can't let them lose now. Bob was running things out there.

There's no-one else to do the job.' He handed his tracksuit to Alex. 'I've been training with the lads,' he continued. 'You know I have. I haven't felt a thing from the knee. Don't look so worried. Find my number. They're waiting.'

The linesman checked Ian's boots and he ran out onto the pitch.

'He'll be OK, won't he?' Joe asked Alex.

'He always was crazy,' said Alex, 'but if he says the knee's OK, I guess we have to take his word for it.'

The stretcher arrived. A white-faced Bob Dixon was arguing with the doctor.

'I told you, I'm fine. I'm not leaving this spot till the end of the game. I don't care what you say.'

Chris looked at Joe's face. He saw the worry there, but there wasn't anything to say. Out on the pitch, Matfield were pulling everyone back in defence. Even Stan Darrowby fell back well inside his own half. Matfield were badly shaken by Bob Dixon's injury.

For a few minutes, it looked as though Haverstone would score. One shot hit the post, and another whistled inches over the bar. Then, gradually, there was a change in the Matfield defence. There was something special about Ian Rawson. Chris could see immediately that he was different from the other players. He would never have believed that one player could make so much difference to a team just by being there – because so far Ian hadn't even touched the ball.

Ian talked all the time, shouting encouragement; and when one of the young defenders made a mistake that led to a close shave, Ian went over to him straight away. The youngster was kneeling on the ground shaking his head, close to giving up. Ian grabbed his hand, pulled him to his feet, and confidence seemed to flow back into him.

In the first half the defending had been desperate; challenges flying in and players getting booked. Now it was very different. Ian stepped forward to intercept a pass. He made it look easy, as if he'd known the ball would be played there. He controlled it instantly with no fuss, and played a simple pass to another Matfield defender. Then as soon as he saw the defender had no-one to pass to, he was there again, ready to receive the ball. The crowd began to shout *'Olé!'* as the Matfield team kept the ball, pass after pass. Matfield couldn't keep the ball all the time, but as the minutes ticked away Haverstone only managed a handful of attacks, and any pass that was played through the middle was cut out effortlessly by Ian.

'How long, now?' asked Alex.

'Five minutes,' said Chris.

'No!' screamed Joe.

The Haverstone striker had finally got through. A brilliant pass had put him past Ian Rawson and he had a clear run in on goal. Ian turned and chased. He gained slowly, but now the striker was inside the area.

'Don't do it!' yelled Alex, but Ian Rawson was level with the striker now, and as the striker raised his foot to shoot, Ian slid in a boot and hooked the ball away to safety. The striker and Ian and the goalkeeper all ended up in a tangle on the ground as the Haverstone players appealed for a penalty.

The ref looked at his assistant on the touchline, and for a terrible moment, Chris thought he was going to give it. Then he blew for a goal kick. Relieved Matfield players patted Ian on the back as the Haverstone players crowded angrily round the ref.

'What a tackle!' said Alex. 'What a player! I'd forgotten, you know,' he said, turning to Joe. 'He would have been one of the great defenders, your dad. You can still see.'

'But he's limping,' said Joe.

'I'm sure he's all right,' said Alex.

'I wish I was,' replied Joe.

Chris watched as the last five minutes ticked endlessly away. He'd seen something he'd never expected to see. There was no question about who was controlling this game. It was Ian. He was like a spider in the middle of a web. Defending wasn't just destroying, like Joe had said. It was something more. And Haverstone were broken. When the final whistle blew, the exhausted Matfield players sat on the pitch laughing in disbelief.

Joe ran straight to his dad.

'Are you OK? Was it your knee?'

Chris could see that Ian was still hobbling.

'I'll get the doctor to check it over. Come on, Joe. Cheer up! We won. Anything could happen now. Wait for me outside the dressing room.'

Mum and Sarah were hoarse from shouting.

'I never thought it would be like that,' whispered Mum. 'Your dad's a star, Joe.'

'He's an idiot,' said Joe. 'Mum's going to go ballistic when she finds out.'

By the dressing-room entrance, Mum found her friend, Jenny.

'Come and have a drink,' said Jenny. 'I don't know whether to laugh or cry.'

'How's your Bob?' Mum asked. 'It looked nasty, that.'

'He's broken his arm,' said Jenny, 'but he doesn't seem to care. He's in there now, talking to the people from the TV.'

Jenny led them towards the bar. Bob Dixon appeared from the changing room. His arm was in a sling.

'I'll be out for the rest of the season,' he said, laughing, as though that was terrific news.

'But what about my dad?' demanded Joe. 'What about Ian?'

'Ask him yourself,' said Bob, as the door opened and Ian Rawson emerged to more cheers from the bunch of fans who were milling about.

'Dad?'

'A crack on the shin,' smiled Ian. 'No problem. The knee's fine.'

Before Joe turned away, Chris saw tears of relief in his eyes. Whatever was wrong with Ian's knee, it must be something serious.

'Come on,' said Ian, 'let's celebrate.'

Everyone in the clubhouse cheered as Ian Rawson and Bob Dixon walked into the bar.

When they had finished, Bob spoke.

'When that ball went in the net,' he said, 'that was the best moment of my life. The doc says there's no way I'm playing any more this season, but I don't care. It was worth it.' A mixture of cheers and groans followed this announcement. 'You don't need to worry,' said Bob. 'We've got Ian, our secret weapon. With him on the team we could go all the way.'

There were riotous cheers at this, but Ian Rawson grimaced as he sat down at the table next to Joe.

'I thought you said you were OK,' Joe accused him.

'I'm fine,' said Ian. 'Just unfit, that's all. I won't be able to move tomorrow.'

'But you can't keep playing, Dad. You know you can't.'

'I can't let them down, not now Bob's injured.'

'But Dad . . .'

'Not now, OK?' said Ian. 'Say goodbye to Bob. Look.'

The ambulance-men had tracked Bob down and were taking him off to hospital. Suddenly everyone was talking at once. Someone brought a bottle of champagne over, and the awkward moment was forgotten in the excitement.

'Well then, Chris,' said Ian. 'Joe tells me you're a natural defender. He says you're good.'

Chris couldn't believe his ears. He looked at Joe, wondering what else he'd said.

'Oh, no,' said Mum, 'you've got that wrong. Chris is a striker. How many goals was it last season? Twenty?'

Chris nodded, embarrassed.

'You can play anywhere then,' said Ian. 'That's even better.'

'The thing is,' said Chris, 'I don't want to be a defender. That is, I don't *think* I want to be a defender. That is, I didn't . . . I just don't know. Everyone keeps telling me I'm a defender suddenly . . .'

'You are what you are,' said Ian. 'I thought I was a winger, until the coach at United persuaded me I was a central defender. Why don't you give it a try?'

'You wouldn't understand,' said Chris.

'Go on,' said Ian. 'Try me.'

Chris looked at the rest of them around the table. They were all chatting away happily, re-living the game. Before he knew it, he found himself telling Ian about Mr

83

Shepherd and the team. It sounded pretty stupid.

'So where's it going to get you then, this stand you're taking? Seems to me you lose all your friends and you don't get to do the only thing you really like doing.'

'Friends!' said Chris, thinking about the scene in the changing room. He wasn't sure he had any friends. Even Gary was against him. 'But I'd have to go back and beg,' he said. 'I'd look like an idiot.'

'Oh yeah?' said Ian. 'So what do you look like now, eh? What have you got to lose, exactly?'

'Hey!' called Chris's mum. 'What are you two looking so serious about? We won, you know.'

Mum was on her third glass of champagne. Everyone in the bar was singing. It turned out there was a Matfield Town song. No-one seemed to know any of the words, but that wasn't stopping them singing. The singing washed over Chris's head. He'd seen two great defenders today; Bob and Ian were the heroes of the Matfield team. He watched the way people came up to Ian and shook his hand, or clapped him on the back. There was something special about being there, right in the heart of things. Maybe

that *could* be him. Then he thought about
what he'd have to go through to get back in
the team, and it was like reality thumping
him in the face. He couldn't do it. There was
just no way.

CHAPTER 9

Sunday stretched empty ahead of Chris. Normally Gary would call round and they'd go to the park. No chance of that. Downstairs, Mum was panicking. She was terrified about starting work tomorrow. To take her mind off it, she was cleaning. The hoover had been going since eight o'clock, with the washing-machine rumbling away in the background. Chris had tried to watch TV, but Mum had shovelled him out of the way. He'd ended up doing his homework. It was a strange sensation, knowing it was there, in his bag, finished.

Even at lunch-time Mum couldn't keep still.

'Sit down, Mum,' said Sarah. 'You're

driving us crazy. You've done most of the jobs on that list already. You'll be exhausted before you start.'

'I feel like those footballers looked yesterday, before the match,' said Mum, picking at her food, 'and if I'm like this now, what will I be like tomorrow morning?'

Chris picked up the empty milk bottles and took them outside. It was one of the jobs on his list. He looked across the street and saw Joe. He was doing something with the flowerpots in his front garden.

'Come on over,' Joe called.

Chris put the milk bottles down and crossed the road. 'Are these what the last people left?' he asked. 'They're mine,' said Joe. 'I grew most of them from seed.'

'Well, they're all dead now.'

'No they're not. Sleeping, more like. I want to get them planted before it gets too frosty. You can give me a hand if you like.'

Chris picked up a pot. It was surprisingly heavy. He followed Joe through the house to the back garden. There were still no carpets or curtains. Boxes were piled everywhere. The sound of an argument echoed from above them.

'I knew this would happen,' said Joe. 'Dad can be totally stupid sometimes. It was bad enough when he told Mum he played yesterday. But when he said he wanted to play in the next round she hit the roof. They've been at it all morning. That's why I'm doing the garden.'

Most of Joe's back garden was grass. Tall leafless trees arched above it, making a kind of tunnel. At the far end was a high brick wall, with a few straggling bushes growing nearby. Joe had dug a flowerbed at one side.

'You're not going to dig all this up?' said Chris. 'It's perfect for football.'

Joe didn't answer. He picked up a spade and began to dig.

'You're crazy,' said Chris an hour later, when he'd helped Joe bury the contents of a dozen pots. He wiped his muddy hands on his trousers.

'I used to help Mum grow vegetables when I was little,' said Joe, 'when we were really poor, after Dad finished playing. I got to like it, that's all.'

Chris saw a plastic football lying under the bushes at the top of the garden.

'Come on,' he said, 'there's plenty of room. We could use the wall at the end for a goal.'

Chris flicked the ball up and kicked it to Joe in the air. He was surprised when Joe hit it back perfectly. They kept it going, back and forwards, until Chris took his eye off the ball for a second and sliced it into the bushes.

'You said you were useless.'

'I am. I can't run, can I? And that's just tricks, keeping it up like that. I'm telling you, in a game, I'm useless.'

'Says who?' demanded Chris. Joe was turning out to be even more complicated than he had imagined. 'You said yourself you can keep running for ages. You can control the ball as well as I can. I bet you can shoot, too. Go on. I'll go in goal and you take penalties.'

Chris was right. Joe *could* shoot. He could head the ball too. He wasn't brilliant, but he wasn't bad either. Then Ian appeared at the top of the garden. Joe picked up the ball quickly.

'There's a drink in here for you,' Ian called.

'I don't understand,' said Chris. 'What *is* all this stuff about being useless? You can play as well as most people.'

'You saw Dad play,' said Joe. 'I'd never be as good as him. I'm not built right. And if I can't be good, I don't want to do it. Anyway, football's not the only thing in the world.'

'That's stupid. You're really into football. You know loads about it. I bet you'd love playing in a team.'

'You mean the team you're *not* in?' said Joe. 'The team you didn't want to be in.'

'That's different.'

'Yeah?'

They stood in silence for a moment. Chris juggled the ball on his foot. 'I've been thinking about it,' he said. 'I can't think about anything else . . .'

'And?'

'I'm going to see Mr Shepherd tomorrow. I'm going to ask if it's OK to go to training.'

'I thought you said they were all rubbish. I thought you didn't want to play with them.'

'Well . . .' Chris was embarrassed. He didn't know how to tell Joe that watching Ian had made him change his mind. 'What about you?' he asked.

'What do you mean, what about me?'

'You could get in the team. I bet you could.' They looked at each other. Then Joe shook his head. 'I don't know,' he said. 'I'll think about it.'

'Get a move on,' yelled Ian from the house. 'It's the draw for the Third Round.'

Chris kicked the ball back into the bushes. It would be brilliant if Joe came to training. Chris had tried to sound confident when he was talking to Joe, but he still wasn't sure he could actually go through with it. He could imagine what the others were going to say. If Joe was there, at least he'd know that someone was on his side.

Inside the house Ian had the radio on, and the teams were already being announced.

'Where's Mum?' asked Joe.

'She's gone over to Chris's. Shut up and listen!'

Manchester United were drawn, and Liverpool, and Arsenal. It began to look as if Matfield wouldn't draw a big team, after all. Then the moment arrived.

'*Number 26 . . . Rainford United . . . will play number 51 . . . Matfield Town.*'

Ian punched the air with excitement. 'North Park! Sixty thousand people! It'll be magic.'

'But Dad, you're not still . . .'

'Wait! Alex is on the radio.'

'*There's not much doubt about the tie of the round,*' the announcer said. '*It just has to be the clash between Matfield Town from the Dudley Morgan Tyres League against high-flying Rainford United. We have Alex Matthews, the Matfield coach, here with us. What do you think of the draw, Alex?*'

'*I'm speechless, John. We couldn't have asked for anything better. It'll be the biggest day in the club's history.*'

'*And a big day, too, for one of your players. Ian Rawson made a miraculous comeback from injury to help your side through the last game.*'

'*Unbelievable,*' said Alex. '*I could never have imagined . . .*'

The phone was ringing in the hall.

'Answer it, Joe, will you? I don't want to miss this.'

Joe picked up the phone. 'Dad . . . Dad! It's for you. It's the radio. They want to talk to you.'

Ian ran to the phone. Chris and Joe sat in the kitchen. They heard Ian's voice twice, in the hall and on the radio.

'*Great to see you back, Ian. You must be over the moon, a big match like this.*'

'I can't believe it's happening,' said Ian.

'*I gather you've come out of retirement just for this Cup run?*'

'This one game, John. That'll do me.'

'*And the old injury? That's all behind you now?*'

'Long time ago, John. They'd have to chain me down to stop me playing in this one.'

Chris looked at Joe. His dad was about to play in the third round of the FA Cup and Joe looked as if someone had just died. Chris heard the key in the door. It was Joe's mum.

'Ian, where are you? Ian? You promised. I thought we agreed. You'd wreck everything for one stupid match. I don't believe it.' She stormed up the stairs. 'Ian? Where are you hiding?'

'Maybe you'd better go,' said Joe. 'I'll see you tomorrow.'

When Stan Darrowby's milk float arrived on Monday morning, it had been painted in Matfield's colours, and people came out from their houses to shake Stan's hand. Everywhere you went in Matfield there were posters, scarves, and flags. The face of Ian Rawson was all over the back pages of the newspapers. *'Rawson's Return'*, it said in the *Daily Comet* that Mum brought home after her first day in her new job.

'How did it go, then?' asked Chris. Not that he really needed to ask. Mum didn't stop talking for half an hour. Sarah made her a cup of tea and she let it go cold while she talked. She told them the complete life histories of everyone who worked in the office.

'But what about Katy?' asked Mum. 'Everyone at work was talking about Matfield Town. She was really fed up last night.'

'Joe says no-one can stop his dad when he wants to do something,' said Chris. 'Not even his mum.'

'That's what Katy said. It doesn't make it any easier though. I don't think I could watch the match, knowing one tackle could put Ian in a wheelchair for the rest of his life. I'm not surprised Katy's angry.'

'Joe never told me that!' said Chris. 'Is it true?' But as soon as he thought about it, he knew that it must be. It explained a lot.

After school on Monday, Chris went to find Mr Shepherd in his room. Mr Shepherd was marking books at his desk. He looked tired, and Chris realized suddenly how young he was.

'Well?'

'I'm sorry about the other night, Mr Shepherd. I've been thinking about it and I . . . well . . . I . . .'

Now that it came to it, Chris didn't know what to say. He could hardly say he wanted to be in the team again. How could he tell a teacher that he'd just discovered how much football mattered to him. It would sound stupid. Mr Shepherd was waiting.

'Is it OK if I come to training?' Chris blurted the words out all at once.

'Sure,' said Mr Shepherd, standing up. 'Don't expect miracles though, will you?'

'I . . . no . . .'

'I thought you'd regret it. And I told you, didn't I? You can't expect to walk straight back into the team. I need to know you're committed.'

'I know,' said Chris. But now that he heard Mr Shepherd say the words, Chris was disappointed. He knew that a part of him had been hoping that he *would* be back in the team. Why not, after all? They needed defenders. And they wanted to win the Cup.

'OK, then. I'll expect to see you on Thursday.' Mr Shepherd turned back to his marking.

All week Chris thought about training. Sometimes it seemed like it wasn't a big deal, but then he'd catch Ranjiv or Phil staring at him and he'd feel like he had a mountain to climb. He didn't talk to Joe about it. All week people kept asking Joe questions about his dad. Joe laughed and joked about it, but Chris could see that he wasn't finding it easy. Talking to Joe about football didn't seem like a good idea. In the end, Ranjiv made Chris's mind up for him.

Chris packed his sports bag on Thursday

morning, still not sure if he could face training. Ranjiv saw him coming through the school gate.

'What have you brought that for?' he said, staring at the bag. 'There's no point you coming. We don't need you.'

'Says who?'

'Everyone. So forget it, right?'

'Oh yeah? You're in charge of the team now? Is that it? Well it would take a lot more than you to stop me.'

'No-one'll pass to you, Chris,' yelled Ranjiv as he walked away.

Chris's anxiety had turned to anger. The anger carried him through the day, and into the changing room. Joe hadn't turned up. No-one spoke to him. He unpacked his things and changed on his own in the corner. He might have been invisible. They ignored him completely. He walked out of the changing room and heard them start talking behind him. Mr Shepherd was waiting.

'You came, then,' he said. 'Good. It can't have been easy.' A fine rain was falling. 'You'd better start jogging. Off you go.'

As soon as he started running, Chris felt better. The misty rain settled in his hair and began to dribble down his forehead. By the time the others started coming across the playground he'd already finished a circuit of the field and he felt as if he could keep on running. Chris heard panting behind him. It was Joe.

'Great,' said Chris. 'You came.'

'I'll never know if I don't try,' said Joe. 'I don't care what Dad says.'

'What *are* you on about?' said Chris.

'He just makes a joke of it,' said Joe. 'How I'm not cut out for it. He's disappointed really. He hoped I'd be like him. You know, follow in his footsteps. There's no chance of that. So I've never tried. But then I thought, why shouldn't I? It's not as if *Dad* pays any attention to what anyone else thinks. So here I am.'

CHAPTER 10

'We're going to work on attack and defence,' said Mr Shepherd. The wind tugged at the soggy pieces of paper on his red clipboard. 'This is the defender's zone.' He waved at an area in front of the goal. 'Attackers; you take it in turns to try and take it past the defender and get a shot in. Chris, you can be first defender.'

Phil muttered something.

'You want to say something, Phil? No? You attack first then.'

Chris was sure he could take the ball from Phil. Something in the way Phil was running told Chris which way he'd go. He won the ball easily, and pushed it back to Pete Johnson.

Pete tried a tricky swerve and stepped

over the ball. Chris stood his ground and watched. Pete kicked his own heels and his legs seemed to tie themselves in a knot. The ball ran forward, out of his control, and Chris chipped it back to the next player. It was Gary.

Gary didn't hesitate. He ran straight at Chris, and he ran fast, but the ball was always under control. Chris froze. He told himself not to back off. He told himself he was better than Gary was, but somehow, with Gary, it didn't work. Gary swayed to the right, and took the ball past Chris with the outside of his left boot. Chris's head cleared a fraction of a second too late. He reacted fast, but his foot missed the ball by millimetres. Gary tripped over his outstretched leg and crashed to the ground. As Gary stood up, Phil rushed forward.

'You did that on purpose.'

'Rubbish! I went for the ball. I nearly had it, too.'

'You were never going to get it. You went for his legs. It's pathetic.'

'It's OK,' began Gary.

'That'll do,' said Mr Shepherd. 'Chris went for the ball.' He turned to Chris. 'You were too slow. Your instincts are good. You should trust them. Sometimes you have to move fast.'

'But, sir.' Phil was still angry.

'Look, whatever's going on between you lot, keep it off the football pitch, OK? Sort it out somewhere else. Now, let's carry on.'

Chris continued defending. He found himself enjoying it more and more. No-one could beat him. No-one except Gary, that was. The next time Gary attacked, he swept past Chris as if he wasn't there. Chris didn't dare make the tackle. If he fouled Gary again they'd all say he was trying to hack him out of the team.

'OK, Gary. You have a go now,' said Mr Shepherd.

'But I'm not playing in defence,' said Gary.

'I want everyone to know how to do every job. If you know what it's like to defend, it's easier for you to see the defenders' weaknesses when you're attacking. A lot of it's in your mind. You tell them, Chris.'

'What . . . ?' Chris stammered.

'Could you take the ball off Gary? Any time you wanted?'

'Well . . . I . . . You know I can't.'

'And how about Pete?'

'Definitely. Every time.'

'Hey!' said Pete angrily. 'You don't know that.'

Mr Shepherd laughed. 'It gives you an

edge, that's what I'm telling you. No-one's saying you can't do it, Pete. It's just that, at the moment, when you take on Chris, he knows he's going to win the ball, and you know it too. It makes a difference.'

Gary took up his position. Pete was first in line.

'Go on, Pete,' Mr Shepherd encouraged him. 'You can do it. Don't get too fancy. Take the ball past him and score.'

Pete ran. He was still angry, and he fixed his eyes firmly on the goal. Gary spotted which side he was going, but he was far too slow with his tackle. Pete picked the ball out of the net with a look of satisfaction on his face, and booted it back to Chris.

Chris hit the ball one side of Gary and ran past him on the other. Gary turned, and it was a race to the ball – a game they had played hundreds of times in the park. Chris won by centimetres, sliding his outstretched foot to turn the ball into the net. He stood up, laughing. And he saw that Gary couldn't stop a smile crossing his face. Suddenly, Chris felt a hundred times better. The feeling lasted until Mr Shepherd organized them into teams for a practice match.

Chris felt stupid, standing on the edge of the penalty area with everyone ignoring him.

And he felt angry too. Gary glanced over at him, but then turned back to talk to the others. Whatever it was that Gary said, the others didn't like it. They all started talking at once, yelling at each other, and at Gary most of all. It was a joke. They were meant to be on the same team: Phil, Gary, Ranjiv, and Chris, with Jez in goal. They were the reds. Chris saw Joe pulling a blue bib over his head.

Phil walked over and lined up in defence, beside Chris. He glanced at Chris, but said nothing. Then the whistle blew, and the blues kicked off. The game was a mess. Chris had no idea what they'd been arguing about, but the result was obvious. Phil wasn't talking to Gary, and Ranjiv wasn't talking to anybody, much less passing to them. He took the ball down the wing, beat Joe, then ran out of space. He turned to come inside, but Joe was back on his feet. When Ranjiv tried to go past him for a second time, Joe tackled him easily. He looked at the ball as if he'd never seen one before.

'Hit it, Joe!' yelled Mr Shepherd.

Joe looked up and saw players running. He pulled himself together and kicked. It was a good pass, right to Andy's feet, but Phil was too quick. He slid in and won the ball. It ran straight to Chris, and he pushed it forward into space. Suddenly the whole of the blue defence seemed to drop away, and Chris felt the blood pounding in his ears as he saw the way clear for a run on goal. He heard Gary calling, screaming for the ball, but one voice rose above all the others. It was Mr Shepherd.

'Give it, Chris! Give it now!'

Chris was torn in two. Every instinct he had pulled him towards the goal, dragged him towards that empty space in the middle of the field. He looked up. There was Gary, waving his arms and yelling. Defenders were closing in. Chris could hear someone behind him. He hit the pass.

It was beautiful. The ball curved right into Gary's path. He didn't even have to change his stride; he drove the ball across the face of the goal, just inside the far post. The reds were ahead.

Chris stood on his own as the others celebrated. Then Gary broke free.

'Great ball, Chris. Brilliant!' Gary was smiling.

'Yeah, good goal,' said Chris. He felt as if something had broken inside him. He couldn't deny it; he'd felt something amazing as he'd hit the pass. In a way, it was as much his goal as Gary's. No. That wasn't right. They'd done something together that neither could have done on their own.

Mr Shepherd stopped the game. 'That was terrific,' he said, looking round at their faces. 'Unfortunately, it was the only good piece of football I've seen today. I told you when we started that you'd have to work hard if you wanted to get anywhere. Part of that is changing your attitude. So far only Gary and Chris seem to be doing that. It was tough for Chris, coming to training today . . .' Chris felt his face reddening.

'And now you're going to put him straight back in the team . . .' said Pete.

Mr Shepherd cut him off. 'As it happens, Pete, the team is the most important thing. And you don't select it.'

Chris was embarrassed at being singled out, but he felt hopeful too. It sounded almost as if Mr Shepherd had changed his mind about him. He was still talking.

'I want to change things around a little. Gary, you swap over to the blues. I want to see how you play with Andy. Pete, you play up front with Ranjiv for the reds.'

Mr Shepherd's instinct was right. Gary and Andy worked brilliantly together. Working in the space behind them, Joe played simple, intelligent passes. It wasn't long before Gary put the ball in the net.

'You should have been with him,' accused Phil.

'He was yours,' said Chris. 'I was trying to mark Andy.'

'If you want to deal with them,' said Mr Shepherd, 'you'll have to work together. Cover each other. Try talking to each other, for goodness' sake.'

Seconds later, Chris won the ball from Andy.

'Get rid of it!' yelled Phil.

Chris looked for someone to pass to. Everybody was marked. Phil wasn't even trying to get away from Gary. He just kept yelling at Chris to pass it. There was nowhere to go but forward. Ahead of him, he could see Pete and Ranjiv. They both started to make runs, trying to lose their markers. Chris took the ball on, into the other half of the field, closer and closer to the penalty area. Then, at last, he saw an opening. Ranjiv was free. Chris went to play the pass, but just at the crucial moment the ball hit a lump of mud. It was only a tiny movement, but it was enough. Chris sliced the pass badly, and a defender picked up the ball.

Chris felt panic sweep over him. He knew

he had to get back, and get back fast. Andy was unmarked, racing towards the goal, and now Gary had the ball, wide on the wing. Phil was chasing Gary, but Chris could see that he'd never catch him. Chris knew he'd have to get to the cross before Andy did. He forced his legs into a last desperate effort. His lungs were on fire. But he was going to do it! Gary hit the cross, and Chris launched himself into the air. His head connected firmly with the ball. He couldn't believe his eyes when he stood up and saw Jez picking it out of the net. He'd scored an own goal.

Ranjiv walked up to him. 'What was that meant to be? You're meant to be a defender. You take a rubbish shot when you ought to pass, then you go charging back and head it past your own keeper.'

'I was trying to pass,' said Chris. 'I wasn't trying to shoot. And I got back, didn't I? It was bad luck, that's all.'

'Come off it,' said Ranjiv. 'Anyone could see what you were trying to do. You haven't changed. You just want to score. You don't even care which goal you score in.'

Chris took a step forward towards Ranjiv, but Gary stepped between them. Luckily, Mr Shepherd was busy, writing on his clipboard.

'Don't be stupid,' hissed Gary. He turned

to face Ranjiv. 'It was an accident,' he said. 'Anyone could see.'

The rest of the game was a nightmare for Chris. His legs grew heavier with every stride he took. Even worse, his passes no longer found his own team, and he started to give the ball away in dangerous situations. He just wanted the game to end. Afterwards, Chris didn't wait to hear Mr Shepherd tell them the team for the semi-final. But before he reached the changing room, he heard footsteps behind him.

'Mr Shepherd,' said Gary breathlessly, 'he wants to talk to you . . .'

Chris's heart started thumping. The others were walking in off the field now, and the rain had started to come down hard, but Chris didn't notice it as he walked past them. Mr Shepherd was picking up a bag of balls.

'You played well,' he said. 'I was very impressed.'

'But I scored an own goal,'

'Everyone makes mistakes. Especially when they're learning a new job. I should know.'

Chris couldn't believe what he was hearing. Maybe he was going to put him in the team. Maybe he'd be sub . . .

'But I'm afraid I can't put you back in the

team for this game, Chris. What you did the other day was wrong. Think of this as a suspension. It's got nothing to do with whether you're good enough. But if you keep working like this, I'm sure you'll win your place back.'

Thanks a million, thought Chris, as he walked away.

'Hey, Chris,' said Gary. He was waiting outside the door of the changing room. 'What did he say?'

'First he told me how good I was, then he said I wasn't in the team.'

'But that's stupid. I thought he'd make you sub, at least.'

'As if you cared.'

'Oh, come on, Chris. Things are different now.'

'Yeah. You're in the team and I'm not.'

'But it was a great goal we scored. Wasn't it? And if we win the semi-final, then you're bound to get back in the team for the final, and with you and me and Andy . . . and Joe's good too. Some of those passes . . .'

'Joe's in the team?'

'Yeah. Amazing, isn't it. I think he's more shocked than anyone else.'

'You make it sound easy,' said Chris. 'You

might want me in the team, but none of the others do.'

'They'll change,' said Gary. 'You'll see.'

'Oh, come off it, Gary. You saw Ranjiv. And Phil. They hate my guts.' Chris felt as if he'd been on a roller-coaster ride. The disappointment was hitting him now. 'We were doing OK until you nicked my place.'

'OK,' said Gary. 'Be like that. I was trying to help, that's all.'

'Gary, wait . . .' Chris swore at himself. He didn't even mean it. Not any more.

But Gary didn't wait. The swing doors crashed together, and Chris stood in the empty corridor trying to understand why everything was so messed up. Then he turned to face the hostile faces in the changing room.

CHAPTER 11

Chris looked out of his bedroom window on Saturday morning and saw Joe leaving his house with his bag over his shoulder. It was nine o'clock, and the curtains in Joe's house were still drawn. Joe closed the front door carefully, opened the iron gate and walked off down the street.

As he ate his breakfast Chris pictured the teams arriving at school. There was always a good crowd for the Cup games. Mums and dads, grandmas, grandads; kid brothers and sisters kicking balls around as they waited for the big match to begin. As Chris thought about the corner flags fluttering, and the nets hung on the goalposts, he felt his stomach twist, just as if he was playing himself. Chris wondered what Joe was feeling.

The house was quiet. Mum and Sarah were both still in bed. Chris went back to his room. From his window he saw Joe's front door open again. Ian came out, yawning, still wearing pyjamas, and picked up the milk from the doorstep. Chris went down the stairs in two leaps, slipped on the rug in the hall, and wrenched the front door open.

'Ian!' he yelled. 'Wait! Joe didn't tell you, did he?'

Ian waited on the doorstep as Chris crossed the road. 'What do you mean? Tell me what?'

'Joe didn't tell you where he was going. Did he?'

'He's gone into town. To buy something or other. I wasn't really listening.'

'He's gone to play football. He's in the school team.'

'Joe? Pull the other one, Chris. He's not even interested. He goes along to training to be with the lads, but our Joe's not a footballer, not in a million years.'

'They kick off at ten,' said Chris.

Ian looked at him for a moment. 'You're serious, aren't you? What a . . . Why didn't he say?'

111

'Search me,' said Chris. 'Are you going to go and watch him, or not?'

'Wait there,' said Ian. 'I'll be two minutes.'

'But I'm not going,' said Chris, when Ian reappeared.

'He's your mate isn't he? His first game. And they're your team. I bet you were thinking about them.'

Chris hesitated. 'I'll have to tell Mum.'

'Ring her,' said Ian, opening the car door and handing Chris his phone. 'Don't just stand there. Get in.'

From the car park they could hear the shouts of the spectators. They rounded the corner of the school with Ian striding out ahead of Chris. He was almost running, but when he reached the edge of the field, he stopped.

'I don't believe it,' he said.

Pete Johnson was under pressure. Pete wasn't small but he looked like he'd shrunk, squashed between two huge attackers. One of them hooked the ball away from Pete, and there was a shout from the Forest Road supporters, but they had reckoned without Joe. He'd seen Pete in trouble and he was waiting as the yellow-shirted attacker brought the ball away. He made a clean, solid tackle, pushed forward into space, and then played a simple pass to Ranjiv.

Ian cupped his hands to his mouth. 'Well done, Joe!' he yelled.

Joe looked round at the sound of his dad's voice. He saw Ian, with Chris beside him.

'Keep it up,' yelled Ian.

'Chris,' said Mr Shepherd. 'I didn't expect to see you here.'

'Hi, there,' said Ian. 'I'm Joe's dad.'

'He's doing OK,' said Mr Shepherd, shaking Ian's hand. 'It must be hard for the lad. A lot to live up to.'

'What did he mean by that?' Ian asked. But Chris didn't answer. He was caught up in what was happening on the pitch. Ranjiv had battled his way out of defence and squeezed a pass through to Phil. Phil set off on a run down the wing, but the defenders pushed him wider and wider. Just when it seemed the ball must run out for a goal kick, Phil somehow curled it back across field. It hit a defender's head and flew out to the edge of the area. Joe was waiting. Chris willed him to hit a perfect volley.

Ian bellowed. 'Hit it, Joe!'

Joe's legs seemed to tangle themselves together. The ball hit his knee and bounced into the path of a Forest Road defender.

Ian sighed. 'I knew it was too good to be true,' he said.

'Oh, come on,' said Chris. 'One mistake. Anyone can make a mistake.'

'You're right,' said Ian. He shouted again. 'Never mind, Joe. Hard luck.'

Joe glanced over to the touchline, then quickly away again. From that moment nothing went right for him. His passes went to the other side, he missed his tackles, and when he fluffed a clearance Forest Road scored. A couple of minutes after that, Mr Shepherd substituted him.

Chris saw Mr Shepherd pat Joe on the back, and then Joe walked off towards the changing rooms. He didn't come over to where they were standing.

'I'm going to go and see Joe,' Chris said to Ian. 'He looked really fed up.'

'*You* told him, didn't you?' said Joe. He chucked one muddy boot on the floor. 'It was great until he arrived.'

'I thought you'd want him to see you play.'

'Well you should have thought a bit harder then, shouldn't you?'

'But he was pleased. He was impressed.'

'I'm not stupid, Chris. I was rubbish.'

'Not all the time. You were doing well when we arrived.'

'Exactly. Can't you imagine what it's like?

I just know that everything I do he could do so much better. It makes me feel useless. Then I *am* useless. He used to make me practise when I was little. I could never do anything well enough. In the end I just gave up.'

There was a shout from outside on the pitch. Chris leapt onto a bench and looked out. Something was happening in the Forest Road penalty area.

'I'm going to watch. Are you coming?'

Joe shook his head. 'I'm going home.'

'So what do I tell your dad?'

'You brought him here. Tell him what you like.'

'What's happening?' Chris asked Ian.

'They've got themselves a free kick. They don't deserve it, though. Look at them, arguing about who's going to take it.'

Chris could hear Mr Shepherd yelling, trying to attract the players' attention. Finally, they heard him. 'Gary takes it,' he shouted. The Forest Road players made a wall. The whistle blew, and Gary ran up and hit the free kick. It went over the wall, hit the bar, and as it fell into the goal a Forest Road defender hooked it clear.

'Goal!' yelled Chris.

'I don't think it crossed the line,' said Ian doubtfully. But the ref had made up his mind. He pointed to the centre spot, shaking his head as the Forest Road players surrounded him.

'Talk about lucky!' said Ian.

'Joe's gone,' said Chris, as the half-time whistle blew. 'He wanted to be on his own, I think.'

'Well I'm staying here,' said Ian. 'I'm enjoying this. I've never really watched kids play before. Not since I was a kid anyway. That Gary's good. The one who took the free kick. Plays a bit like Paul Scholes. But some of them won't pass to each other. It's crazy.'

'Tell me about it,' said Mr Shepherd, coming up behind them. 'They seem to play against each other as much as they play against the other team. Joe did well for his first game. He's a bit disappointed, being taken off, but he'll get over it. At least our luck's holding.'

Ian started to say something, then stopped. 'Yeah,' he said finally, 'I guess you're right.'

The second half began. Parkside couldn't get out of their own half. Gary and Phil were spending all their time defending, and when the ball was cleared upfield there was no-one to chase it. As the game went on it seemed inevitable that Forest Road would score.

'They need someone to take the pressure off,' said Ian. 'Someone to think a bit. Look at that. Sheer panic.'

Ranjiv had won the ball. As three attackers closed in on him he tried to pass to Gary, and succeeded only in laying on a perfect ball for the nearest of the attackers.

'Come on, Parkside,' shouted Chris. 'You can beat this lot.'

Ranjiv turned to see where the shout had come from. Chris saw a surprised look cross his face. Then he turned away and raced back into the action. The Parkside supporters started to make a bit more noise, and the tired players seemed to move a little more quickly.

'Yes!' called Ian. 'You can do it!'

The game was nearly over and the scores were still level when Ranjiv finally managed to get a decent ball to Gary's feet. Gary was just a couple of metres inside the Forest Road half, and Forest Road had two defenders back. The situation looked hopeless. Chris glanced at the Forest Road goal. The keeper was laughing at something a spectator had said to him. He was right on the edge of his area.

'Hit it, Gary,' Chris yelled. He knew Gary could do it. It was one of the things they'd practised in the park. Gary looked up and saw the keeper.

'Go on!' shouted Chris and Ian together. Gary hit the shot. It flew high in the air and seemed to float there. The keeper realized too late what was coming towards him and started back-pedalling furiously as the ball began to drop. It hit the crossbar, rebounded onto the back of the goalkeeper's head and trickled into the goal.

The Parkside fans leapt in the air, shouting and cheering. Forest Road hardly had time to kick off again before the final whistle went. Chris watched the team celebrating the win, and shaking hands with the Forest Road players. He could even hear Mr Shepherd saying, 'Brilliant! Well done all of you!' Suddenly, he felt empty. He didn't want to be there any more.

'Can we go?' he said to Ian.

'Sure.' Ian looked at his watch. 'I'm going to be late. Matfield are playing Wolfits Biscuits "A" team this afternoon.'

'You're not playing?'

'I might have a little run out for five minutes.' Anger flashed briefly in Ian's eyes. 'I'm not a kid, you know. I don't need people telling me what to do.' Privately, Chris thought Ian seemed very much like a kid.

Ian laughed. 'Look, I know Joe and Katy are worried about me, but I do know what I'm doing.'

'Chris. Hey, Chris!' Gary had run after them. 'Thanks, Chris. I'd never have spotted him off his line if you hadn't shouted. I told Mr Shepherd. I told him we need you in the team.'

Ian laughed. 'Player power,' he said. 'And what did your Mr Shepherd say to that?'

'He said he'll decide after Christmas,' said Gary, 'but he's bound to put you back in. We were dead lucky to win that, and Joe . . .' He stopped, embarrassed.

'Joe's good,' said Chris. 'You wait and see.'

'Yeah. OK. Look, I've got to get back. I'll see you, Chris. Mr Rawson.'

It didn't matter what Gary said. Chris had seen the others looking at him. Even if he did ever get back in the team, it wasn't going to be any fun. But he knew as he watched them straggle happily back across the field that he wanted to be part of it. And he wanted Joe to be part of it too. He had to say something to Ian.

'Joe's scared of you,' he said. The words came out in a nervous rush.

'You what?' said Ian.

'He's scared of what you'll think. He's scared he won't be good enough; that you'll think he's rubbish.'

'I won't. I wouldn't. How could I? He's my son, isn't he?'

'But I saw you,' said Chris. 'When Joe messed up that shot. If he'd been one of those Matfield defenders in the Cup, you would have been helping him, wouldn't you? That's what makes you so brilliant when you play. But you didn't do it for Joe . . .'

Chris stopped. He felt himself reddening. Ian had gone very quiet. He didn't speak again on the short drive home. Chris let himself into Number 28, and found Sarah crying quietly at the kitchen table.

CHAPTER 12

'What's up then,' said Chris. 'Trouble with your boyfriend?'

Sarah didn't have a boyfriend, but when she cried it was usually about a boy she wanted to go out with. He knew this was different when she didn't throw anything at him.

'Shut up, Chris,' said Mum. 'Leave us alone, will you? We'll have some lunch in a little while.'

Chris went into the hallway. As he closed the door he heard Sarah say, 'I still miss him, Mum. I know it's stupid, but I can't help it.'

'I'm sorry, love. I can't change the way he is. He thinks he can do what he likes and

121

then make it all better with money. You know what I think.'

'I didn't think I minded. Then when he promised to take me out and he didn't come, I knew I did. I know you hate him, Mum, but he is my dad.'

Chris was astonished. Sarah and Mum had always been against Dad. He thought back. He'd never heard either of them say one good thing about Dad. The way Sarah talked most of the time, you'd think she wouldn't care if she never saw him again. Chris hadn't spoken to Dad since that night after football training. He felt cold suddenly, remembering the things he'd said. *I don't want your help. I wouldn't come if you paid me.* Maybe it was his fault Dad hadn't taken Sarah to Alton Towers. And now Dad was in London.

Chris sat down at the computer and began to make a team: Jez in goal, Ranjiv and himself in defence, Joe, Pete and Phil in midfield, Gary and Andy up front. Then he added Sol Campbell, Zinadine Zidane and Michael Owen. They should beat anyone. He settled down to play the Champions League. But it was no fun. He couldn't stop thinking about Sarah, and Mum, and Dad.

*   *   *

Two weeks later school broke up for the Christmas holidays. There was no more football. It poured with rain for a week and then froze solid. They could have played ice hockey on the football pitch. On the last day of term, Miss Jones handed Chris a brown envelope.

'Make sure it gets there,' she said, smiling. 'It's not bad news this time.'

'This'll do instead of a Christmas present,' said Mum when she opened it. 'Getting dropped from the football team was the best thing that could have happened, if you ask me.'

'That's not why my work's better.'

'No? What then? You'd better think of a good reason, or I might be tempted to stop you playing football for ever. Oh, Chris! You should see your face. I'm joking.'

The next morning the Rawsons went away for Christmas. The whole street seemed empty and quiet with them gone. He'd been spending a lot of time with Joe, playing on the computer, or helping him clear out the old greenhouse in his garden. But the best thing had happened on the day after the match against Forest Road . . .

Ian had appeared in the garden with a football.

'OK, then, you two. You both need some practice, so let's go. Matfield have hired the indoor pitch at the Sports Centre, but we're not starting till eleven o'clock, so there's a couple of hours free. Come on.'

'No thanks,' said Joe. 'I'll stay here.'

Chris was amazed that Joe could be such a laugh at school, and be like this with his dad. He looked at Ian, and saw that he was hurt. Ian was really trying to help.

'Please, Joe. Even if you just go in goal. I bet there's loads of things your dad can show me that I don't know.'

Joe reluctantly put down the trowel he was holding.

'Great,' said Ian. A smile lit up his face. 'Let's go.'

Ian stood at the centre of the empty pitch, juggling the ball. Chris pulled on his trainers and ran out to join him. Ian flicked the ball to him and they began to pass to each other, keeping the ball in the air. Joe took a long time in joining them. When he did, Ian pulled the ball down on to the ground and passed it to him.

'Let's just pass it around,' he said. 'Dead simple. Try to flick it on first time if you can. If not, take a touch.'

Doing something so simple, it was easy to concentrate on getting it right. And even doing something so simple, it was hard to do it as well as Ian did. It didn't matter how awkwardly the ball came to him; he was always ready to move it on perfectly round the triangle. Joe started to relax. Chris knew that Ian was making it easy for both of them; making sure he gave them easy balls to control. When he flicked it into the air and started giving them high, bouncing passes to deal with, they always came in the perfect spot, just right for the chest or the thigh or the head.

'OK, then,' said Ian to Chris, 'let's do some work on tackling. What do you do when an attacker's running at you? Joe, you go in goal.'

Chris watched Ian coming towards him. Ian stepped over the ball and feinted to go left. Chris glued his eyes to the ball. He saw Ian's foot moving, preparing to push it to the right. Chris lunged. Everything seemed to blur. Ian was past him, and Chris didn't know how he'd done it.

'As soon as you commit yourself, you give the attacker his chance,' said Ian. 'You have to be certain you're going to win the ball if

125

you dive in like that. But there's plenty of other things you can do. Am I right-footed or left-footed?'

'I don't know,' stammered Chris.

'You need to know,' said Ian. 'You watch most players, even the top professionals, they have one foot better than the other. You can force them to go the way you want them to go. Then if they do get in a shot or a cross, it's with their weaker foot. You can usually see straight away.'

'So which *is* your best foot?' asked Chris.

'Both,' grinned Ian, 'but then, I'm special. Come on, let's do some work.'

In the hour that followed, Chris learned more than he would have thought possible. And most of what Ian told him had nothing to do with kicking a football.

'Sure,' he said, 'sometimes you have to make a great tackle, or hit a great pass. But the most important thing is being first to the ball. And you do that by thinking. Watch what's going on, figure out how the other side work, and never stop concentrating.'

'And there's one more thing,' he said, as they walked to the car. 'I watched that team of yours yesterday, and there's some good players. But they don't talk to each other. One shout from you, Chris, and Gary scored a fantastic goal. If you get back in that team, you make sure you talk to them.'

Chris thought about this later. It was one thing to imagine himself back in the team. The way Ian talked, he was supposed to tell them all what to do. That was just stupid.

Chris was looking forward to Christmas. Sitting on the shelf in the kitchen were tickets for the FA Cup. Rainford United against Matfield Town. The game was right at the end of the Christmas holiday, and Ian had arranged everything. Sarah was seriously excited about that. She'd be seeing Selim Volkan play. Also, Gary had called round a couple of times. Things weren't exactly the way they used to be, and Chris could see that they'd never be friends again in quite the same way they had been before. But at least Chris knew that Gary wanted him in the team.

'Don't worry about the others,' Gary had said. 'Everyone says things they don't mean when they get mad.' Chris knew very well how true that was. 'It's not just you anyway,' Gary went on. 'They're always falling out with each other. And with me. You saw them the other day.'

Chris felt a lot better when he thought

about what Gary had said. Things were definitely getting better. Then Christmas Day arrived.

'I haven't had time to buy you anything,' said Mum, handing envelopes to Chris and Sarah, 'but I expect you'll prefer this anyway. And I earned it all myself.' There was a lot of money in the envelope. 'You deserve it,' said Mum, when she saw Chris's face. 'You've been working really hard at last.'

Then there was the present from Dad. Inside the parcel was *Demon Attack*. Chris was about to shout *Yes!* when he saw Sarah's face. She had a coat in her hands.

'He doesn't know anything about me any more. Does he, Mum? No-one could wear this.'

'Open mine,' said Chris. 'Go on.' He handed her the long parcel covered in sellotape. Chris had never had the patience to wrap parcels properly. Sarah tore the paper off and unrolled a giant poster of Selim Volkan. 'You'll be seeing him play in a couple of weeks,' Chris explained, 'but I thought that would keep you happy until then.' Before he could get out of the way Sarah had grabbed hold of him and kissed him on the cheek. Chris turned bright red, and escaped to his room to load the new game.

*　　*　　*

It was four o'clock when the phone rang. Mum answered it.

'Hello, Colin,' Even today, on Christmas Day, her voice went cold and hard. She passed the phone to Chris. 'He wants to talk to you.'

Sarah got up and walked out of the room.

'Hello,' said Chris.

'Happy Christmas,' said Dad. Chris could hear loud voices in the background, and glasses, and music. It sounded like a pub.

'Yeah,' said Chris.

'You like the game?' asked Dad. 'It's an import, you know. It's not out here yet.'

'Yeah. It's great. Thanks.'

'Oh, come on, Chris. Lighten up a bit. It's Christmas. How's the football? Has the new coach seen the light yet?'

'Not exactly.'

'This is like talking to a brick wall. Look, I'm sorry if I screwed up with the PE teacher, OK? And I've got news for you. I've got tickets to see Tottenham. Guess when? Go on.'

'I don't know,' said Chris. 'Next month?'

'Tomorrow!' said Dad. 'I'll drive up and collect you. Let me speak to your mother.'

Chris glanced across the room. Mum had

disappeared into the kitchen. Chris took a deep breath.

'What about Sarah?' he asked.

'What do you mean, "What about Sarah?" She hates football.'

'I mean, how come you take me out all the time, and not her? Like you come and watch me play football and she's not supposed to know. It's not fair, Dad.'

There was a silence at the other end of the phone.

'Well?' said Chris. 'Dad?' Dad started to say something, but Chris ignored him. 'I don't want to go and see Tottenham. I don't need you telling me how to play football. Why don't you take Sarah out instead?'

'But where? Anyway, she wouldn't want to, not on her own.'

'How do you know? Have you asked her? Don't hang up. I'll get her.'

'Chris, wait . . .'

'Sarah!' yelled Chris. 'Dad wants to talk to you.'

Five minutes later Sarah came out of the front room in a daze.

'He's going to take me out,' she said, 'On my own. We're going shopping. In London.'

Then she burst into tears.

CHAPTER 13

Two weeks later Chris was in the back of Mum's new car on the way to Rainford. Joe sat beside him in the back seat, and Sarah was in the front. Ian had left very early that morning, and although it was now only ten-thirty they had already heard him interviewed twice on the radio. They had tried to persuade Katy Rawson to come with them, but when they left she was levering the lid from a pot of paint.

'I'm staying indoors. I'm not listening to the radio; I'm not answering the phone. One thing I will say, though. This is the last time.'

There were dozens of cars travelling up the motorway with purple and orange scarves flying from the windows. It seemed as

131

though the whole of Matfield was on its way to Rainford. Mum had bought the car a week ago. It was very old, and it made some puzzling noises, but it seemed to go, and Mum was singing as she drove along. Sarah joined in. She was wearing the new jacket she'd bought on her expedition to London with Dad. He had rung up a couple of times since then just to talk to her.

As he gazed out of the window at the passing countryside, Chris thought about the training session the week before. He hadn't done anything special, but he'd tackled well, and he'd managed to ignore the stupid comments from Pete and Ranjiv. He felt as if he was starting all over again, living his own life for a change. At the end of the session, Mr Shepherd had announced the squad for the final. Chris was in, and so was Joe. Some of the others had looked doubtful, but Chris was sure now about what he wanted. He wanted to be a defender. A defender like Ian Rawson. Not a hacker or a destroyer, but the one in the middle, the one who makes things happen.

He glanced over at Joe. Joe had been pleased to be picked, but Chris could see he was worried about Ian. It seemed crazy. Ian was so fit, so skilful, but Joe insisted: all it needed was one badly-timed tackle and Ian's leg could be seriously injured – for good this time.

'He won't listen to anyone,' Joe had told him. 'He's hardly ever at home. He spends all his time at the gym, or running. It's like he imagines he's eighteen again.'

Two hours later they came over a hilltop and saw Rainford in the valley below them. Rainford was a big town, almost a city. There was no chance of getting lost though. They followed the cars in front and ended up in a gigantic car park. Above the roofs of the nearby buildings, the floodlights of North Park rose into the sky.

'Cheer up, Joe,' said Chris, as they walked through the crowded streets towards the ground. 'It's going to be great. It's like something out of a film. Ian Rawson's comeback. If he really thought it was dangerous to play, he wouldn't be doing it, would he?'

'You don't know my dad. It's glory he wants. That's what he always wanted, only he never got it. Now he can see a chance. It's not just a game to him. It's everything.'

The capacity of North Park was sixty thousand. Three thousand Matfield fans fitted into one small corner of the ground, but they made enough noise for ten times that number. When the teams ran out onto the pitch the sound was deafening.

'There he is,' sighed Sarah. 'Selim Volkan. He's wonderful!'

'We haven't come to watch him,' said Chris. 'Look. There's Ian. He looks great, doesn't he, Mum?'

'I must say, he does look very fit. I think you should stop worrying, Joe, and enjoy the game.'

A little further along the stand, the radio commentary team were preparing for the kick-off.

'*We're here at North Park*,' said the commentator, Alvin Brown, settling deeper into his sheepskin coat, '*for what has to be the tie of the third round. Little Matfield Town of the Dudley Morgan Tyres League take on the might of Rainford United, riding high in the Premiership. What do you think, Sandy? Can they do it?*'

'*This is the FA Cup*,' said Sandy Mackay, a craggy ex-footballer. '*Anything can happen. But if Ian Rawson wasn't there, I'd have to say no. He's the man who could make the difference here. I played with him, you know. Could have been one of the greats.*'

'*A tragic story, Sandy. But maybe this will be the happy ending. If they pull it off it*

*will be one of the great Cup upsets. And
they're ready to kick off now.'*

The moment the game began, Chris forgot
all thoughts of Ian's injury. When he glanced
at Joe, he saw at once that it was the same
for him. Surrounded as they were by the
fierce emotions of the thousands of Matfield
fans, they could think of nothing but the
struggle that was going on out on the pitch.

Rainford kicked off. Their team was full of
stars, and on any other day Chris would have
been thrilled just by the sight of them. He
knew what they could do. He saw them every
week on TV. The front two were fearsome.
They had already scored thirty goals
between them in the league this season –
Derek Bradford and Steve Brennan. Rainford
stroked the ball around the pitch. They were
in no hurry. The skill of the players was
beautiful to watch. The Matfield players
chased and tackled, but whenever one of
them did win the ball, there always seemed
to be a Rainford player ready to step in and
start another move.

'Why don't we attack?' asked Mum.

'We haven't got the ball,' said Joe. 'Don't
worry. Dad knows what he's doing. How
many shots have Rainford had?'

'None,' said Sarah.

'Exactly,' said Joe.

'But they only need one,' said Chris.

'They'll get complacent,' Joe told him. 'You can see it already. Sooner or later they'll go for it. They'll push too many men forward and we'll hit them on the break.'

'This isn't the blood and thunder Cup-tie we were led to expect, Sandy,' said Alvin Brown.

'Dull. That's the word I'd use, Alvin. The—'

'Hold on, though. United are attacking with more purpose here. Great pass from Knightley. Bradford's dummy. He's left it for Brennan. Great control from Brennan. Must be a goal. But what a block from Rawson! How did he manage to get to that?'

'First real bit of goalmouth action we've seen, Alvin. Great play from Ian there. He hasn't lost his touch. But it looks like United have decided it's time to stop messing around.'

'Here they come again. Terrific ball down the wing. Pulled back to Brennan. Brennan plays a lovely reverse pass. He's fooled everyone. No! Rawson read it. He's got the ball. United are over-committed here. Great run from Darrowby! He's taken two defenders with him. It's all opening up for Rawson.

136

They're backing away, letting him run. Darrowby's screaming for the ball now. But it's a shot from Rawson. Oh, what a goal! That one just screamed into the net. And the Matfield fans are going crazy!'

Ian Rawson ran all the way back down the pitch to the Matfield supporters.

'You did it, Dad! You did it!' Joe screamed the words over and over again. Ian stood below them, arms raised high in the air as the crowd cheered, on and on. The rest of the ground was silent. Ian couldn't hear Joe shouting. Joe knew that, but he kept on shouting anyway, until the ref ran over and pulled Ian away from the crowd.

Now that Matfield were ahead, United threw everything at them. The game was played at a frantic pace, but somehow Matfield hung on until half-time. The crossbar was rattled twice by fierce drives from Bradford, and Brennan hit the post. When the Matfield players came off the pitch, they were clearly exhausted.

'This is where the gulf in class begins to show, Sandy,' said Alvin Brown. *'You can't expect a bunch of part-timers to be as fit as top professionals.'*

'The part-timers are winning though, Alvin.'

'*They won't be for much longer, but I will say this. We've a real Cup-tie on our hands now.*'

When the second half began, Chris felt more nervous than he'd ever felt in his life. Matfield started well. Ian seemed to have figured out the United attack, and he'd obviously spent the interval giving advice to the young defenders around him. United found it impossible to get crosses in, and Ian cleaned up everything that they played through the middle. The minutes passed, more slowly than Chris could have imagined possible. There was no doubt that United were on top. There was no doubt that they were the better team. But with just fifteen minutes left, it began to look as if the impossible would happen, and Matfield would go through.

Then Selim Volkan picked up the ball in midfield. All the Matfield players were back in their own half, but somehow Volkan picked out Brennan with a curling pass.

'*Great control from Brennan,*' said Alvin Brown. '*He's got his back to goal, though, and Ian Rawson's marking him tightly. Brennan spins. Great piece of skill. And Rawson's slipped! Brennan's away. Yes! That's the equalizer. At last.*'

'Ian Rawson's down,' said Sandy Mackay. 'Looked like he turned awkwardly to me. Where's the replay? See how his leg went from under him? They're calling for a stretcher.'

'Well, Rawson doesn't want to go. He's getting up. But they're making him get on the stretcher. The game's re-started, and Matfield only have ten men on the field. Alex Matthews, the Matfield manager is arguing with Rawson. It looks like they're taking him to the dressing room. But Matthews isn't making the substitution yet.'

'My guess is, they're getting a doctor to look at that knee,' said Sandy.

Chris turned to talk to Joe, but Joe had gone. He was at the end of the row. And now he was racing towards the entrance of the stand.

'Joe!' yelled Chris. 'Wait!'

Mum grabbed his arm, but Chris pulled it away, and before she could say anything, he had gone, racing up the steps after Joe.

CHAPTER 14

The echoing corridor underneath the stand was empty. Chris looked both ways, and then he heard Joe's running footsteps. Above him, the crowd roared and sighed. He ran fast, and as he emerged from the darkness, he saw Joe only fifty metres away.

'Joe! Wait. Where are you going?'

Joe paused. 'I'm going to see Dad. He was going to play on. I know he was. They'll never stop him. I'm going to make sure he doesn't carry on.'

Joe ran past the high brick wall at the end of the main stand and out into the street. There were a few police officers here, waiting for the end of the game. The door of the player's entrance was firmly locked. Joe hammered on it, but no-one came. As he raised his fist to knock again, the door opened suddenly. A tall man wearing a blazer and a Rainford United tie looked angrily down at them.

'What do you think you're doing? Clear off before I call the police.'

'My dad,' said Joe. 'I've got to find him. Before it's too late.'

'His dad's Ian Rawson,' said Chris. 'Please listen. His dad's been injured.'

'Right. I warned you.' The man stepped into the street and waved at a nearby policeman. Joe didn't hesitate. He slipped past the man and in through the door, with Chris close behind him.

A long corridor stretched ahead of them. At the end, there was a flight of stairs. They ran past empty offices and down more stairs. Joe stopped, confused. Angry shouts came from the corridor behind them. Then they heard more voices. Clear, and very close by.

'Don't be ridiculous. It's nothing. I twisted it when I fell. I've got to get back out there.' It was Ian. The door marked VISITORS was right behind them. Joe crashed into the dressing room. Ian was lying on the treatment couch and the United doctor was probing his knee with his fingers. Sid Black, the Matfield trainer, was standing beside him.

'Joe, Chris. How on earth . . . ?'

'Tell him to stop,' Joe said to the doctor.

'I've been trying,' said the doctor, grimly. 'He's not done any serious damage, but he'd be a fool to carry on. Only he insists that he knows best. There's nothing more I can do, I'm afraid, short of chaining him to the table.'

Ian swung himself off the couch and put his feet on the floor. Chris saw him wince. Then he headed for the door. Joe was crying. Chris took two steps and stood in front of Ian.

'You can't,' he said. 'It's not worth it.'

For a second, he thought Ian was going to hit him.

'You don't know anything,' said Ian. 'All my life I've been waiting for this. I thought the chance had gone. I'm not letting a dodgy knee stop me. They'll lose out there without me.'

Still Chris stood in front of Ian. It's true, he thought. Probably they will lose. But he didn't move.

'Come on,' snapped Ian. 'Get out of the way.' He took a step forward, and gasped with pain.

'You can't,' said Chris. 'And anyway, you won't be any use to them like that. Will you?'

Ian stopped. Chris saw that there were tears in his eyes. He looked helpless, like a child. He turned, walked back and sat heavily on the couch. He put his head in his hands. After a few moments he looked up.

'I'm sorry, Joe,' he said. 'I don't know what's been happening to me.' Ian was shivering, as if he was freezing cold. 'I thought I could do it, I really did. I thought it was a miracle – that the doctors had made a mistake and there really wasn't anything wrong with my knee. Or it had got better somehow. Then, out there, just now – well, you must have seen. It just went. I knew right away what it was. I just . . .' Tears were running down his cheeks. He hugged Joe.

Sid coughed. 'You're not going back on then, Ian? There's only ten men on the field. We've got to move.'

Ian shook his head. Sid turned and ran from the room. Only then did Chris notice the United official and the police officer, standing by the door. 'It's OK,' said Ian. 'They're with me.'

Ian limped slowly down the tunnel holding Joe's hand. Chris walked beside them. They came out onto the pitch the same way the players did, under the famous sign that said, THIS IS NORTH PARK. And suddenly they were in the middle of a volcano of noise. A reporter thrust a microphone in Ian's face.

'What's the news on the knee, Ian? I see Jason Harvey's coming on.'

'My knee's OK,' said Ian. 'But after what the doc told me in there, I'd be crazy to carry on. Now, if you don't mind, we're still in a match out here.

'I think you'd better get back to your mum,' he continued to Chris, 'and take Joe with you. She'll be wondering where you are.' He spoke quickly to the yellow-coated steward standing nearby, and the steward walked with them past the United bench.

Chris could have reached out and touched the players. Half of them were internationals. There was Ruut van Basten, and Gianlucca Poppi. A bellow from the United manager nearly splintered Chris's eardrum. Then they were past, and there was Jason Harvey, waiting with the referee's assistant. Alex Matthews was yelling instructions in his ear.

Ian put an arm around Alex Matthews and drew him away from Jason. 'Let me talk to the boy,' he said.

'Stop,' said Chris to the steward. 'Let's just see Jason go on.'

It was easy to see that Jason was terrified.

From down here on the touchline the stands towered above them. With only ten minutes left, United were hurling everything at Matfield, and the noise of the crowd was deafening. Yet through it all Chris could still hear the sound of three thousand Matfield fans yelling, 'MATFIELD! MATFIELD!'

'Listen,' said Ian to Jason. He had to shout to make himself heard above the noise, so Chris heard every word. 'You don't need to remember anything. Forget whatever Alex was saying. You've probably forgotten it already. This is the best day of your life. You may never get another chance like this. Go out there and enjoy yourself.'

The ball went out for a throw. Jason smiled, and ran out onto the pitch in front of sixty thousand screaming fans.

'*Rawson's not carrying on,*' said Alvin Brown. '*This lad is Jason Harvey. Eighteen years old, and most of the week he's a plasterer. Let's see what he can do against the most prolific scoring partnership in the Premiership.*'

'*United are very dangerous in the last ten minutes of any game,*' said Sandy Mackay. '*With Ian gone I wouldn't be surprised if they bang a couple in.*'

'*Here they come now. Brennan's made one*

of those fabulous diagonal runs. Volkan
hits a curling ball down the wing. Brennan
crosses it first time. Bradford, surely. Oh,
that's a terrific header from the boy, Jason
Harvey. Must have been taking lessons from
Rawson.'

'I'm sure he has, Alvin, but he's going to
need to be really good to stop these two.
They're on fire!'

Chris watched from his seat in the stand.
In all the noise, there was no way he could
make Mum understand what had happened.
He thought Jason was brilliant. To go out
there, at Rainford Park, in front of sixty
thousand, and play like that. And he was
eighteen. Eighteen didn't seem too far away
to Chris. That could be him out there, in a
few years' time . . .

The ninety minutes were nearly up. All
around him, the Matfield supporters had
begun to whistle.

'It should be over,' Mum yelled in his ear.
'Why doesn't he blow the whistle?'

'Added time,' said Chris.

'He can't just add time.'

'It's for when Ian was injured,' yelled
Chris. 'Look!'

The ref's assistant was holding up a board.
Five minutes of stoppage time.

'I can't bear it,' said Sarah.

On the touchline, Alex Matthews shouted frantic instructions to his players.

'Forget it,' said Ian. 'There's nothing you can do now. They can't hear you.'

'But we're so close,' shouted Alex. 'Stan!' he screamed. 'Mark him! Get back!'

Bradford had the ball. Stan Darrowby forced his tired legs into a final effort, chasing back to try and force Bradford into a mistake. Bradford was moving forward towards the edge of the area. Jason was ahead of him, like a brick wall.

'No, Stan!' Jason shouted, but it was too late. Stan was already sliding in to make the tackle.

'Free kick!' shouted Alvin Brown. *'And it's right on the edge of the box. Perfect position for Brennan.'*

'That was never a foul,' said Sandy Mackay, watching the replay. *'He took the ball. Look at that.'*

'He took Bradford's legs as well. Both of them. And he's going in the book. Now then. What's happening here? Looks like Volkan fancies this one. There's a pretty heated discussion going on down there. The ref wants the wall back the proper distance. The Matfield players are going to spin this out as

long as they can. And it's going to be Volkan who takes it. Here he comes.'

'I can't watch,' said Sarah.

'Neither can I,' said Mum.

Selim Volkan ran up and hit the free kick. The ball seemed to have a life of its own. It rose up over the wall and seemed to change direction in mid-air before flying just inside the post. The Matfield players collapsed on the ground as the whole United team raced away to celebrate. Rainford were in front and there were only seconds left to play. The entire stadium erupted in a blaze of green and white. Only the Matfield corner was quiet. Tears were running down Sarah's face.

'How could he do it to us?' she said, 'How could he?'

Then someone nearby began to chant, 'MATFIELD! MATFIELD! MATFIELD!' The noise grew. More people joined in. Before long, all the Matfield fans were shouting, chanting, singing and yelling. The noise was fantastic. The Matfield players picked themselves up, and turned to applaud their fans. And then Stan Darrowby kicked off. It was the final kick of the game. As the ref's whistle blew, spectators all round the stadium stood and cheered. Rainford United had won. The

United players shook hands with the Matfield players, and their manager led them off the pitch in triumph. The Matfield team ran to their supporters. The noise in the ground was incredible, and it seemed to be growing. The United fans were cheering the Matfield team! Chris saw Ian pointing, saying something to the rest of the players and they set off on a lap of honour. Everywhere in the ground the United supporters stood and applauded them.

An hour after the game finished the Matfield fans were still there. It was like an enormous party. Gradually, the Matfield players joined them. They all had friends and relations there watching. Joe saw Ian limping along the side of the pitch.

'Dad! Over here!'

Ian fought his way through the crowd. Everyone wanted to shake his hand. He looked quiet and serious.

'I'd like a lift home with you,' he said to Chris's mum, 'if that's OK?'

In the car, he tried to ring Katy. There was no reply.

'She'll be painting,' said Joe. 'Mum always does what she says she will.'

'I'm going to burn that poster of Selim Volkan when I get home,' said Sarah. 'I don't

149

care if it was a present. I'm going to get a poster of Jason Harvey.'

'Don't be like that,' said Ian. 'It was a great day. Wasn't it?'

Ian and Joe climbed out of the car in Raidon Street. Their house blazed with light from the curtainless windows. They crossed the road and Katy stood in the open door. Chris watched as Ian and Joe hugged her. Then they went inside.

CHAPTER 15

As Chris stood on the soggy football pitch at Parkside Middle School the excitement of North Park seemed a long way away and a long time ago. It was raining, and very cold. It was Thursday night – the last training session before the final of the Inter-Schools Cup – and things weren't going well.

'The semi-final was hard,' Mr Shepherd was saying, 'and you were a bit lucky, to say the least. The final will be a lot harder. Some of you look to me like you just don't care.'

Right now, that was exactly how Chris felt. The game at Rainford had been magic. That was the only word for it. And the more times Chris replayed the game in his imagination, the better it became. There was no magic here. Mr Shepherd made them work and work. Passing, shooting, dribbling, heading. But when they played, nothing seemed to connect. Even Gary looked depressed. Only Joe was cheerful.

That was because, on the far side of the pitch, Ian Rawson was huddled in an old anorak, hugging himself against the cold. He didn't look much like a superstar, and most of the others hadn't even noticed him, but Joe had. And to Chris's amazement, when his dad had arrived Joe had started to play better. All of Joe's anxiety about his dad watching him play had disappeared. It was Chris who was now feeling the pressure.

Chris had spent Sunday morning removing the strikers from his bedroom walls and ceiling. Pinned to his cupboard door he had just one picture now – Ian Rawson making a headed clearance in front of a bank of Rainford United supporters. And now he knew just how Joe had felt. Ian Rawson was over there watching everything he did.

At the start of the session, some of the others had nodded hello to him. They hadn't exactly been friendly, but when they'd started playing, at least they had passed to him – at first. That was when the pressure had begun. There was Ian, over there on the touchline, watching. And there was another Ian too, a small voice inside his head: *'Keep it simple. Watch the game. Use your instincts. Offer yourself for the pass. Talk to them . . . talk to them . . . talk to them . . .'*

He had made mistake after stupid mistake, and gradually the others stopped passing to him. He stared at the mud between his boots as Mr Shepherd reorganized the teams.

'Pete, Chris, you stay back. You can move between the edge of your own area and the halfway line, but that's it. Ranjiv and Phil, you fetch and carry in midfield. Gary, you're the striker, but you also help out in midfield. You'll have a lot of running to do. I want to see you talking to each other, calling for the ball. Do it.'

Chris forced himself to try. He stayed in position. He made space for himself. He called for the ball. But still no-one passed to him. He made a good, solid tackle and won the ball. He played a simple pass to Pete, and ran for the return, but Pete turned away from him and passed to Ranjiv. Chris called again, but still the ball didn't come. The wind was getting up, and the rain had turned to sleet. It was blasting horizontally across the pitch. Then someone from the other team played a long ball down the middle.

'Mine!' yelled Chris, running to make the interception. 'I've got it.' He ran, keeping his eyes on the ball as it fell towards him.

CRUNCH!

'That was mine,' shouted Pete, holding his head.

'I called,' Chris yelled back. 'I had it covered.' His legs were tangled with Pete's. They both tried to stand up together, and fell towards each other.

'Get off me,' hissed Pete.

Chris lashed out. All his frustration went into the punch, but it never landed. Joe caught his arm.

'Don't be an idiot. You'll wreck everything.' He turned to Pete as Mr Shepherd came towards them. 'That was Chris's ball,' he said. 'We're playing Church Road in two days' time. If we don't sort this out it'll be a disaster.'

'If they're not going to pass to me,' said Chris, 'then there's no point me being in the team.'

'That's right,' said Pete, 'there isn't.'

'What on earth is going on here?' demanded Mr Shepherd. 'Every time I leave you lot for a few seconds, there's trouble.'

'It's OK,' said Gary. 'It's sorted out.'

'No it's not,' said Pete and Chris together.

'Excuse me,' interrupted Ian Rawson. 'Tell me to shove off if you want. But I might be able to help here.'

'Be my guest,' said Mr Shepherd. He looked disgusted.

Ian pushed back the hood of his top and the rest of the boys realized who the stranger was.

'It's happened to me,' said Ian. 'Two players going for the same ball. You both shout "mine" and you smash into each other. I even got in a fight once, and . . .' Mr Shepherd coughed. 'Yeah, well,' Ian went on, 'that's another story. The point is, accidents happen. You have to forget it. Get on with the game.'

'Let's face it,' said Gary. 'It's not just Chris. We're all playing rubbish.'

Chris looked gratefully at Gary.

'That's right,' said Ranjiv. 'We've done all this training and we all seem to be getting worse.'

The others nodded.

'We were dead lucky in the semi-final,' said Pete. 'If it hadn't been for Gary we'd probably have lost.'

'And who spotted the chance?' said Gary. Pete glanced at Chris and shook his head.

'I can't believe this,' said Ian. 'I've seen what Mr Shepherd's been trying to get you to do. He's right. You all play like you're the only one on the park. If you do pass, it has to be to your best mate. You need to get real. I've played with people and I've hated their guts. But you have to forget all that when you get on the pitch. You can't waste time looking for your best mate to pass to. Think about what you're trying to do. You're trying to win the Cup, aren't you? And there's no way you and your best mate are going to do it on your own, is there?' Chris looked around at the others. A lot of them were looking sheepish. No-one could look Ian in the eye. 'Give it to the first man you see who's unmarked,' Ian continued. 'It really is that simple. Do that, you'll be amazed at what starts to happen.' He put his hood back up and walked off.

'Well,' said Mr Shepherd, 'what are you waiting for?'

Right away, things began to improve. Almost at once, Pete hit a short pass to Chris. Chris had got so used to Pete trying to find Ranjiv that he was nearly caught out. He killed the ball and hit it crisply back to Pete, then moved for the return. When it came, Chris didn't have to think. He knew

exactly where Gary was, perfectly pos-
itioned, and he hit the pass first time. Gary
had his back to goal. He controlled the ball
and laid it back to Ranjiv. Then he turned
past his defender as Ranjiv struck the
through ball. Ian and Mr Shepherd
applauded from the touchline as Gary's shot
hit the back of the net.

'Better!' called Ian.

'Much better,' agreed Mr Shepherd. 'Keep
that up and we might have a chance.'

'How do you feel now, then?' asked Ian. He
was driving Chris and Joe home. They sat in
the back, still recovering from the cold.

'Nervous,' said Chris and Joe together.

'Good,' said Ian. 'It shows you care. For a
moment back there, I saw some real football
being played.'

'It won't last,' said Chris. 'You don't know
what they're like.'

'Rubbish. Some of you really looked like a
team. It's a great feeling, when you all start
playing together. I'm going to miss it.'

Chris caught the sadness in Ian's voice.

'But you can watch,' he said. Even as he
said the words he knew that watching wasn't
the same. 'You can watch Joe. You can watch
us win the Cup. We'll make up for Matfield

losing. It'll be as good as winning the FA Cup.'

'Sure,' said Ian. 'It'll be great.'

'How did it go?' asked Sarah. She was on her knees by the fireplace in the front room. Her Selim Volkan posters were in a pile on the floor.

'Bad, then worse, then a bit better,' said Chris. 'What are you doing with those?'

'I was going to burn them. But he *is* gorgeous. I feel like a traitor.'

'I wouldn't worry. It's over now. Burning Selim Volkan's picture won't wipe out his goal.'

'Hmmm,' said Sarah, gathering up the posters. 'You're right. And they cost a lot of money, too.'

Chris threw himself into a chair and switched on the TV. A wave of doubt swept over him. For five minutes they'd felt like a team, but that wasn't enough. All last year he'd played with the same players, but the way they treated him now, he might as well be a total stranger. Then, suddenly, images came crowding into his mind – images of himself – images of Chris Jackson, the striker. It was as if he was looking at someone else – someone he didn't like very much. He replayed game after game from last season in his mind. Until now, Ranjiv's words had just been words. *It's you. You never get back and help*. Now, at last, he saw himself the way others saw him. He felt sick, but at least he knew one thing – he wasn't like that any more. And he'd never play that way again.

'Chris?' He hadn't realized that Sarah was still there.

'I said I'd ask. I mean, Dad wanted to know . . .'

'What?'

'I don't know what happened between you. He didn't say. But it's better to make it up. Really it is.'

'So what *did* he say?'

'Why don't you ring him? He says he did something stupid. I think he's embarrassed . . .'

'Come off it.'

'But you want him to see you play, don't you? He's always been there. He never used to miss a game, did he?'

'But . . .'

'Your secret? Come on, Chris. You don't really think we didn't know? Give him a ring.'

When Sarah had gone Chris sat for a long time, thinking. Then he picked up the phone.

'Hello.'

'Dad?'

'Chris? . . . Sarah told me about all the excitement. Matfield, I mean. And your new neighbour. I saw the game on TV. Dead unlucky.'

'Yeah.'

'Sarah told me you're back in the team. Well done.'

There was a silence.

'Chris? Are you still there? Can I come and watch you play? Is that OK?'

'You never asked before. You always just turned up.'

'No. I never thought. Sarah says you're going to play in defence. She says you want to. Is that right?'

'I know what I want to do. No-one's made me do it. But I have to do it on my own.'

'Your new neighbour been giving you a few tips, then? That must be great.'

'Not really. Well, a bit maybe.'

'So you don't want me to come and watch?'

'No. I mean, I don't know. You'll just watch, you promise? You won't try to tell Mr Shepherd what to do?'

'I promise. So when is this big match?'

'Saturday. We're at home. Ten o'clock. But,

Dad, you mean it? You'll just watch? You know Mum'll be there?'

'It's sorted, Chris. Between Mum and me, I mean. Don't worry. And Chris – about Sarah. Thanks. Her and Mandy got on like a house on fire.'

Chris put the phone down slowly. Mandy. Sarah. Sarah had met Mandy. They must have all gone shopping together. Mandy had always been just a word in Dad's mouth until now. It had meant nothing. Now Dad was in London. Living with her. He hadn't said so, but Chris knew. And Sarah had met her. Chris's world seemed to heave itself up and rearrange itself. For so long he'd been pretending. Nothing was how he had thought it was. He'd been pretending Mum and Dad would get back together. Now, suddenly, he *knew* it would never happen. And then another, surprising thought came to him. It didn't matter. Not any more.

CHAPTER 16

The banks of fans seemed to rise for ever under the floodlights. Chris couldn't understand why Parkside were playing the final here at North Park. He heard a yell. It was Alex Matthews. He was jumping up and down on the touchline. Chris started walking towards him.

'No!' yelled Alex. 'Get back! Get in position!'

'But I'm only a boy. I shouldn't be here. I can't.'

'Too late. Look out.'

Chris turned. Steve Brennan was running at him. Chris started to run, but he felt his feet slipping. He looked down. He was wearing slippers. And pyjamas. Steve

162

Brennan was growing. He had claws . . . and
fangs . . . He was blocking out the light . . .

Chris sat up in bed, panting as though he'd
been running a race. Moonlight filtered in
through the bedroom window. He looked at
his clock. Three-thirty. He'd escaped from one
nightmare into another. Six and a half hours
to go to kick-off. He'd never worried about a
game before, but since Thursday night the
anxiety had grabbed hold of him, and it
wouldn't let go. He knew he should sleep, but
he couldn't. He dozed restlessly until it began
to grow light. Then he took a folder of news-
paper cuttings from his drawer.

One of the papers had reprinted stories
from ten years before. There was a picture of
a young Ian Rawson jumping for a high ball.
He was twenty years old. The paper was
tipping Ian for a place in the World Cup
squad the following year. Two weeks after
the article was written, Ian had been
injured. A year later, as England played in
the World Cup, Ian had given up the struggle
against injury and retired from football.
There was another picture of Ian kicking a
ball to a toddler. It was Joe.

Chris looked out of the window, thinking

about what Ian had lost. And Ian was still a great player. He'd been brilliant in the two games Chris had seen him play. Ten years ago, fully fit, he must have been the best. And there he was now, right across the street, getting the milk in. He looked up, saw Chris's face in the window and waved. Chris opened the window and a gust of freezing air swept into his room.

'Can't sleep?' Ian called across. 'You don't have to tell me. Listen, you can do it. I know you can.'

Chris shivered, and felt better. At breakfast-time, he even managed to force some cereal down.

'Are you ready then?' said Mum. She was putting her coat on. So was Sarah.

'You're both coming?'

'Of course.'

'I thought you only liked the legs,' Chris said to Sarah.

'I sort of enjoyed the football too. Amazing, isn't it? And you *are* my brother. And it is the Cup Final.'

'I just hope you won't be disappointed, that's all. We haven't exactly been playing brilliantly.'

As they got into the car a few flakes of snow began to fall.

*   *   *

When they pulled into the Sports Centre car
park, the first thing Chris saw was Dad's car.
Sarah jumped out and ran over. Dad hugged
her, and the two of them walked back
towards Chris and Mum.

'Hello, Colin,' said Mum. Chris looked at
them – his mum and dad. Dad kissed Mum
on the cheek, and she let him. Chris couldn't
believe his eyes.

'Hi, Chris,' said Dad. 'Ready for the big
game?'

Chris looked past Dad to his car. The
passenger door was opening, and a woman
was climbing out. It had to be Mandy.
Suddenly, Chris just wanted to get away.

'There's Joe,' he said. 'I have to go. I'll see
you later.'

Chris glanced back as he reached the
changing-room door. They were all shaking
hands and talking. Chris felt his heart
thumping. It had never crossed his mind
for a moment that she'd actually come here.
And there was Mum, shaking hands with
her.

'Hey, Chris! Come on.' Joe tugged at his
arm. From behind the door he heard the
sound of voices arguing. It was almost a
relief. Joe opened the door, and walked into

the middle of a shouting match.

'You only pass to Ranjiv,' Gary was saying.

'Nuts,' said Pete. 'I pass to you. I pass to Phil.'

'Not if you can help it,' said Andy.

'So what about you?' shouted Pete. 'If you can't pass to Gary, you just go for goal. You never look for anyone else.'

'We've got an understanding,' said Andy. 'If you can't see that you're more stupid than I thought.'

'Shut up!' Chris yelled. 'Shut up all of you.'

There was an astonished silence. Chris was as shocked as anyone else. He felt as though someone else was talking.

'They'll walk all over us if we're all arguing like this. You know what Ian said. We'll be beaten before we start.'

'He's right,' said Jez, who had been sitting quietly in the corner. 'We've been lucky to get this far. But this lot are different. Some of their players have had trials with big clubs. There's this kid called Billy Miller. He's been in the papers.'

'How come you know all this?' said Pete.

'I'm the one who has to stop the shots,' said Jez. 'I take it seriously, even if you lot don't.'

The door opened and Mr Shepherd walked

166

in. The tension crackled in the air. 'OK,' he said. 'Let's go.'

Snow was falling steadily as they ran out onto the pitch, big wet flakes that rested for a moment on the grass and then melted slowly. The team from Church Road Middle School were already on the field. Chris looked for the striker, Billy Miller. He'd remembered as soon as Jez had said the name. He'd seen his picture on the back page of the *Matfield Gazette*. And there he was, a tall, skinny black boy, hitting practice shots at the goalkeeper. Ian's words came back to Chris – *Watch which foot he uses*. Chris watched closely. Billy Miller was hitting shots easily, but almost all the time he used his left foot. Just as Chris was making up his mind, Billy trapped the ball with his thigh and hit a right-footed volley. He didn't seem to put a lot of effort into the shot, but it streaked past the keeper before he could get a glove to it.

'Hey, come on, Billy!' yelled the keeper. 'That nearly took my head off.'

Billy Miller grinned, and hit a beautifully judged chip with his left foot that floated over the keeper's head.

'That soft enough for you, Fingers?' he asked. Chris watched for a few moments longer. *He's left-footed*, he decided finally, *but he's pretty good with his right as well.* He jogged over to where Joe was standing.

'You OK?' he asked him.

'Not bad,' said Joe, 'but after what went on in there, I reckon we've got no chance. Look at them.' He pointed to the Church Road players playing head tennis in the centre circle.

Gary ran up. 'You ready, then?' he asked. Chris nodded. 'I know we can do it,' said Gary. 'I've got this feeling. I know it seems bad. Everyone arguing like that. But I reckon all that training we've done has really made a difference.'

Chris looked doubtfully at the sullen faces of the rest of the team. Only Jez was smiling as Andy hit him practice shots. Chris looked at Gary. His oldest friend. He couldn't believe how much Gary had changed. His confidence was infectious, and Chris found himself grinning, in spite of the sick feeling in his stomach. On the touchline, Mum and Sarah were standing with Dad and the woman who must be Mandy. Ian was there, and Katy was with him.

'Your mum's here,' Chris said to Joe.

'She says it's the first match she's watched for ten years,' said Joe.

'Let's make it a good one, then,' said Gary, as the referee blew his whistle. Gary was the captain. He ran off towards the centre spot. 'Good luck,' he called over his shoulder.

We'll need it, Chris said to himself, as he took up his position in the centre of the defence.

Church Road Middle School weren't just good – they were top class. That's what Chris told himself five minutes later when the ball went out for a throw-in. Even their kit was better than Parkside's. From the kick-off they had put together an amazing sequence of passes. Every Church Road player had a touch of the ball before Pete finally managed to get a foot to it and force it out for a throw.

'We might as well give up now and go home,' Pete muttered. Chris didn't have time to answer. He had Billy Miller to deal with. Miller was coming at him now. The ball was at his feet, and he looked supremely confident. He was grinning at Chris, looking him right in the eyes. Chris wrenched his eyes away. It was the ball he needed to watch. Billy swayed to his right. *'No!'* said a voice in Chris's head; *'He won't go that way.'*

It happened very fast, but to Chris, time seemed to slow right down. He saw Billy step over the ball. He stayed calm. He saw Billy make his move, swerving left, touching the ball forward. Chris struck, and suddenly time started again. Chris had the ball. Billy was surprised, but only for a second. He spun on his heels, ready to tackle back, but Chris was too quick. He played a short pass to Pete, and sprinted forward. Pete stopped the ball neatly, but two attackers were closing in.

'Yes!' said Chris, turning back, offering himself for the pass. Pete played the ball. Chris had made it easy, and now Ranjiv was in space to his left. Chris passed. Ranjiv controlled it and moved the ball on to Phil, who was running ahead of him.

'That's good, Parkside,' yelled Mr Shepherd. 'Keep it up!'

'Man on!' shouted Chris, as a stocky midfielder closed on Phil. 'Get rid of it.' Phil glanced behind him, and panicked. He hit the pass in a hurry, and the ball ran straight to the feet of an opposition defender.

'Hard luck,' Chris called. 'Nice try.'

He didn't wait for Phil's response. Billy Miller was on the move again.

As the first half drew to a close, Chris felt a growing sense of satisfaction. Church Road had had almost all of the possession, but they'd managed only two shots on goal, and

170

neither of those had come from the left foot of Billy Miller. Every time Billy had forced himself into an attacking position, Chris had managed to move him out to the right, and it was clear that Billy preferred his left foot. His right-foot shots were both on target, but Jez dealt with them comfortably. Even better, Parkside Middle School were playing like a team at last. Not a brilliant team, maybe, but they were definitely working together. Then disaster struck.

Ranjiv had made a brilliant tackle out on the left wing. Chris could see that he was just beginning to believe in himself. Ranjiv played a good solid pass to Joe, and Joe, as usual, did the simple thing well. He laid the ball off to Andy, right on the halfway line. All at once Chris realized that Parkside had a real chance. He could see Gary's flashing diagonal run. If Andy could just pick him out!

'Andy!' Chris shouted. 'Give it to Gary!'

Andy looked up and saw Gary's run. The pass looked perfect. It was drilled between two defenders, right into Gary's path. The trouble was, it was Gary's first touch of the game. Normally, Chris knew, Gary would have hit the shot first time, but now he took a fatal extra touch, and that was enough for a defender to steal the ball.

The speed of the counter-attack was bewildering. Suddenly, black and yellow players were streaming out of defence like a swarm of angry bees. There was a pass from a defender, long and straight, and the winger was racing down the right. Billy Miller was sprinting flat out towards Chris. If he was fast with the ball at his feet, he was dynamite without it. Chris tried to keep his eye on the winger, too.

'Close him down, Pete,' he yelled.

Pete nearly made it. Nearly, but not quite. The winger wrapped his left foot around the ball and sent it curling across the penalty area. Chris saw the ball, but he had lost Billy. He didn't know where he was. Chris hurled himself at the ball, but even as he flew through the air he saw that Billy was airborne too. He saw the whole thing. Somehow Billy twisted in the air, pulled back his head, and nodded the ball deliberately past Jez's despairing fingers and into the net.

CHAPTER 17

Chris could taste the cold earth in his mouth. He could hear the Church Road supporters celebrating. Then he felt a hand on his shoulder.

'That was tough. No-one could have stopped him.' It was Ranjiv.

'I should have hit it first time,' said Gary. 'If I had, we'd be one–nil up.'

'I should have stopped him getting that cross over,' said Pete.

'Don't be stupid,' said Chris. 'He was just too good, that's all. There was nothing any of us could have done.' Chris stood up. 'There's only a couple of minutes to half-time,' he said. 'Let's just hold out till then.'

A storm of yellow and black attacked them. Church Road were keen to kill the game before half-time. Parkside pulled everyone back and, somehow, they survived.

'I'm proud of you,' said Mr Shepherd as they sucked at their drinks.

'But we're losing,' said Chris.

'And we've only had one shot on goal,' said Gary.

'Yes, well, I've been talking to Mr Rawson about that . . .'

'Ian,' said Ian.

'We're going to have to take some risks if we're to get back on terms. We're going to have to get men forward from midfield, or even from defence.'

'But we can't,' said Chris. 'You've seen Billy Miller. You can't leave him unmarked for a second.' The others murmured agreement.

'You don't have to,' said Ian. 'If one of you sees an opening the others cover for him. Sure, it's a gamble, but if you don't gamble now, you've no chance.'

'But none of us could handle Billy,' said Ranjiv. 'Even Chris got beaten in the end. What chance have the rest of us got?'

'Don't worry,' said Chris. 'I'll cover Billy. I'm enjoying it, in a funny sort of way.' Chris felt his face reddening. He was pleased, but embarrassed at the same time.

'It doesn't matter who gets forward,' said Ian. 'It's surprise that counts. If any of you see an opening, just go for it. The rest of you cover. You're doing great by the way. You're a credit to your coach.' He slapped Mr Shepherd on the back, and it was Mr Shepherd's turn to go red.

There were a few moments left before the game re-started. The snow had stopped, and the sun came through the clouds briefly, making the wet grass sparkle. Chris looked around at the faces of the team. There was no arguing, no laughing or joking. Everyone was serious, intent.

'Chris?' It was Dad. 'Hard luck on that goal. You nearly made it.'

'I didn't, though,' said Chris.

'It's only one goal,' said Dad. 'You can win it. I know you can.'

The whistle blew.

'Chris!' yelled Gary. Still Chris stood there as the snow drifted down again.

'Go on,' said Dad. 'You can do it.'

Chris turned and ran onto the pitch. 'Come on Parkside,' he yelled. 'Let's take them apart!'

For fifteen minutes the game balanced on

a knife-edge. The quality of the football was amazing. From his position in the heart of the defence, Chris watched Parkside turn into a real team at last. The players who had been at each other's throats half an hour ago were helping each other now. Whenever Chris had the ball there were always two Parkside players calling for it. They were tightly marked but gradually they began to find ways of making themselves a metre of space, half a second more time. And the best thing for Chris was the way that Joe was playing.

As the minutes passed, Joe came into the game more and more. He seemed to grow stronger as the relentless pace of the game drained the strength from the others. He began to find not just one metre of space in midfield, but two or three. And his control was excellent. He could kill the ball instantly, turn, and be ready with his pass. Slowly, very slowly, Parkside began to dominate the game.

On the touchline, Ian Rawson turned to Katy. 'Joe's doing great, isn't he?'

Katy nodded. 'Katy?' Ian said. 'What's the matter?'

'It's Chris,' she told him. 'I mean, look at him. Who does he remind you of?'

Ian squeezed her hand. 'I know,' he said. 'I knew it as soon as I saw him kick a football. He's just like me.'

It was true. And Chris's confidence was growing all the time. It was obvious to all the spectators that Chris was winning the battle with Billy Miller. Chris was cutting out everything that came through the middle of the defence. Gradually he was forcing Billy to withdraw deeper and deeper, simply to get a touch of the ball. The next time there was a break in play, Chris said to Ranjiv, 'I can cover you. Ian's right, we have to take a risk. If you see a chance, go for it.'

Ranjiv looked at Billy Miller. He was bent double, trying to get his breath back after another fruitless run.

'OK,' said Ranjiv, slapping Chris's hand. 'You're on.'

Seconds later, Ranjiv won the ball on the edge of the penalty area.

'Go!' yelled Chris. Ranjiv looked up. He pushed the ball forward and began to run. He ran slowly at first, then, amazed at the space he was being given, faster and faster. The Church Road players were yelling at each other.

'Mark him, someone.'

'Go to him, Gerry.'

But all the time, Ranjiv was moving forward. Joe crossed in front of him, drawing one defender away to the wing, and Gary darted into the area, taking two more defenders with him. Ranjiv hesitated.

'Go on,' screamed Chris. 'Blast it!'

Ranjiv blasted it. His shot hit the back of the net before the goalie could move. The Church Road players hung their heads as Parkside celebrated, but Chris didn't waste time on celebrations. He ran the length of the pitch to pick the ball out of the net, then he ran back and placed it on the centre spot. As he took up his position again, Ranjiv beamed at him.

'Don't get carried away,' said Chris. 'We haven't won it yet.' Then he grinned. 'Brilliant goal,' he said. But even as he spoke, Church Road were on the attack. Billy Miller played a one-two with another attacker. Parkside just weren't ready for him. When Ranjiv had scored, most of them had started to imagine victory, and now it looked as if all their hard work could be undone in a matter of seconds. Chris's legs seemed to be moving too slowly. Billy played another pass. Joe reached out to try and intercept, but even he was too slow, and Billy moved swiftly on to the return. Chris saw him coming. He forced himself to think, but Billy Miller in full flight was a truly terrifying sight. Chris backed off; he couldn't help himself, and before he knew it, he was on the edge of his own area.

Chris knew he had to prevent Billy from getting in a shot with his left foot. He moved to block Billy's path; to force him to the right, where Ranjiv was waiting. But, somehow, Billy had got his second wind, and with it a devastating burst of speed. He seemed to slide sideways, and drift two metres forward into the penalty area in the blink of an eye. Chris knew he had to make the challenge. There was no choice. He slid in, eyes fixed on the ball as Billy pulled back his boot, and felt relief wash over him as he hooked the ball to safety. He couldn't believe his ears when he heard the referee's whistle. He looked up and saw him, arm in the air, whistle in his mouth, pointing to the penalty spot.

Instantly, Chris was on his feet, shouting. He couldn't stop himself.

'I never touched him!'

The ref shook his head. 'I know what I saw, young man. So don't make matters worse.'

'You must be blind,' shouted Chris, as

Gary dragged him away, still protesting.

'Right,' said the ref, 'your name's going in the book. I advise you to say no more.'

'Calm down,' Joe urged him, as the ref wrote laboriously in his notebook, and then held up the yellow card. 'You won't help anyone if you get yourself sent off.'

'He didn't touch me, you know.' It was Billy Miller. He had crashed to the ground, badly winded. Now he was facing the ref. 'It was a great tackle, that's all.'

'Has nobody told you about arguing with the referee? You're in the book, too, sonny. My decision is final.'

'But . . .'

'So who's taking this penalty, then?'

Billy looked at the ref. Then he looked at Chris. 'Sorry, mate,' he said to Chris, and he placed the ball. The whistle blew, and Billy ran up. He hit the ball as sweetly as a penalty could be hit. He hit it with his left foot, high to Jez's left. But Jez had moved early. He was already airborne, the outstretched fingers of his left hand reaching for the ball. He made it, but only just. The ball took the smallest of deflections, and smashed against the crossbar.

For a second, everyone stood still and watched the ball. No-one could believe what had happened. Only afterwards did they discover that Jez's homework on Billy Miller had included finding out from his cousin at Church Road which way Billy hit his penalties. The Parkside supporters gasped with relief. The Church Road supporters gasped in disappointment and astonishment. The Church Road players had their heads in their hands. And in the middle of it all, only Chris stayed cool.

He saw nothing but the ball. He moved decisively and took it on the turn, flicking it round a stunned attacker with the outside of his boot.

'Out!' he yelled. 'Gary, Andy, Joe! Move!'

Chris raced forward with the ball at his feet. Too late, the Church Road players realized their danger. Chris hit a curling pass out to Joe on the wing. Joe had five metres start on the defender who should have been marking him. It was enough.

'Go on, Chris!' called Pete. Chris hesitated. Then he heard Ian's voice from the touchline.

'Get in the area, Chris. Go on! They're all over the place.'

Chris raced forward. Gary was over to his left, and there was Andy beyond him. Both had defenders at their heels. Joe looked up and crossed the ball. It was perfect. Chris felt the old, familiar surge of blood that told him he was going to score.

And then, in the instant that he was going to hit it, he knew there was a better choice. He didn't see the defender, but somehow, he knew he was there. He knew where Andy was too. And Gary. Electricity seemed to crackle down his spine. At the last possible moment, when all the defenders were committed, when the goalkeeper had already started to come out, Chris opened his legs and let the ball flash between them.

For one terrible second, as he waited for the sound of Gary's boot thumping the ball into the net, Chris thought he'd got it all wrong. He'd fooled everyone. Maybe he'd fooled Gary too. He turned. Gary had brought the ball down. He hadn't volleyed it. Chris's heart missed a beat. *Stay cool, Gary*, he thought. *Please!*

Gary leant back and chipped the ball. It seemed to float up for ever, over the hands of the advancing keeper, beyond the outstretched leg of the last defender, and dropped gently into the goal.

As Chris and Gary were buried by a pile of bodies, the final whistle blew.

It was all over. Parkside had won the Cup.

CHAPTER 18

Chris barely heard Mr Shepherd's excited congratulations. He hardly saw the faces of the dejected Church Road players as he shook hands with them. He was stunned by the perfection of the goal. He'd seen players do it on TV – dummy the ball and watch it fall perfectly at another player's feet – but he could never have imagined how it would feel. He could still see Gary leaning back – chipping the ball . . .

'Here you are, son. Well done!' A man was offering something to him. Everything was blurred for a second, then came suddenly back into focus. A medal. His medal.

'Thanks,' he mumbled. He took the medal

183

and joined the others as Gary lifted the trophy. There was a loud cheer from the spectators, and at that moment the real world came flooding back. There was Mum and Sarah, and Mum's friend, Jenny, and Bob Dixon with his arm in a sling, and Ian and Katy. Dad was standing there, cheering as loud as anyone else – and *she* was standing beside him. It was crazy. Now, when he should have been celebrating, Chris felt as bad as he had felt before the game.

'Fantastic, Chris,' said Mum, as the crowd broke up and excited knots of families and friends surrounded the players. 'You were brilliant. You were all brilliant.' Mum kissed him. Then Dad was there, and *she* was beside him.

'This is Mandy,' said Dad.

'I've waited a long time,' said Mandy. She held out a hand. Chris took it. There wasn't anything else to do. His heart was beating very fast. He found himself looking into a pair of serious brown eyes.

'I thought you did really well,' she said. 'And that was never a penalty. I thought it was an excellent challenge.'

'I . . .' Chris stopped. This wasn't what he had expected. What *had* he expected?

He didn't know. She was looking at him, waiting – and smiling now. She wasn't a monster. She seemed completely normal.

'Mandy's a bit of a football fanatic,' said Dad. 'She's a Tottenham fan. Never misses a game.'

'Yeah, but I'll tell you what,' said Mandy. 'That was the best goal I've seen all season.'

Chris felt himself going red. 'Don't,' said Dad. 'You're embarrassing him.'

'No,' said Chris. 'It's OK.' It was as if a wall which had been blocking out the light for years had just been demolished. The moment he'd been dreading had arrived, and now it was gone. And it wasn't bad; it was good. He realized he was going to like Mandy.

Much later, Chris was sitting down at the kitchen table with Mum and Sarah when the doorbell rang. They had just waved goodbye to Mandy and Dad, and Chris suddenly felt exhausted. The celebrations after the game had been brilliant, but now that he was home again he could hardly keep his eyes open.

'It's Ian,' said Sarah. 'He wants us to go with him. He says he's got a surprise.'

Ian followed Sarah into the room. He laughed when he saw Chris struggling to wake up. 'Come on, Chris,' he said. 'One last effort. It'll be worth it, I promise. Then you can sleep for a week.'

Joe and Katy were waiting in the street. 'What's going on?' Chris asked Joe. 'What's the big secret? Where are we going?'

'Search me,' said Joe. 'But Mum's in on it, whatever it is.'

Chris got in the back of Mum's car and they followed Ian through the back streets.

'I know where we are,' said Chris suddenly. 'We're going to the Matfield ground.' Sure enough, a few minutes later they turned into the industrial estate. They drove past the tractor factory, and there was the ground in front of them. The Matfield Town sign had been repainted, and the cracked concrete at the front of the building was covered with fresh black tarmac. Ian was getting out of his car with an enormous grin on his face.

'OK,' he said, opening the door of the club-house. 'This way, everyone.' He led the way into the bar where they had celebrated the victory over Haverstone. 'I'd like you to meet the new manager of Matfield Town.'

'Where?' said Chris. The room was empty.

'Ian,' said Katy. 'Just tell them.'

'It's me,' said Ian.

'But you can't be,' said Joe. 'What about Alex Matthews? What about Mum?'

'It's OK, Joe,' said Katy. 'I've given up. I've never managed to keep your dad away from football anyway. He's never really wanted to do anything else, and all those dead-end jobs just made him miserable. He had to make me one promise, that's all.'

'That's right,' said Alex Matthews, emerging from his office. 'Ian Rawson is most definitely *not* a player-manager. He's played his last game for Matfield. And as for me, I'm going to be far too busy looking after all the building work to manage the team. Here, take a look.' He unfurled an enormous sheet of paper on the table. 'This is the new stand that we're building with the money from the Cup,' he said, pointing to the plans.

'But what's this?' said Chris. The plans didn't just show one stand. They showed a whole new stadium.

'We're thinking big,' said Alex. 'Why shouldn't Matfield have a decent football team?'

'It already has,' said Mum.

Alex laughed. 'Well, a decent football team

needs a decent stadium,' he said. 'A capacity of ten thousand in two years' time, that's what we're aiming for.'

'And by that time,' said Ian. 'I'm aiming to take us into the Football League. And what's more, we'll have our youth programme up and running. In five years, we'll be in Division One. In ten years . . .'

'Ian Rawson!' said Katy. 'You're crazy! You're completely mad!'

Everyone was laughing, but Chris could see that Ian really meant it. And at that moment, Chris knew that it could really happen. After all, who would have thought Parkside would win the Cup? Who would have thought that Chris Jackson would turn into a defender? Who would have thought that Matfield would nearly beat Rainford United at North Park? And who would have thought that, just half an hour ago, he would have been sitting round the kitchen table with Mum and Sarah and Dad and Mandy and they would all have been smiling and laughing together?

Chris could see it all. The new stands rising where the old rusting buildings stood now. The floodlights blazing down, and thousands of fans cheering as the teams ran onto the pitch. And maybe he would be there too, a defender, right in the middle of everything. Chris looked into Ian's shining eyes, and he knew that anything – absolutely anything – was possible . . .

THE END

TROUBLEMAKERS
by Paul May

Tough enough for the team?

Robbie is desperate to try out for the school
football team. He's full of raw talent, skilful
and agile, with terrific co-ordination.
So why does everybody reckon he's
got no chance.

Chester Smith is a top-class professional
United player. But his game is falling to
pieces, and now he's faced with a continual
barrage of ugly taunts from ignorant
hooligans in the crowd . . .

Then Robbie and Chester meet, and it could
be the beginning of a new chance for each
of them. If only they can avoid the
troublemakers . . .

An action-packed football tale,
Troublemakers is hard-hitting, realistic
and inspiring.

SHORTLISTED FOR THE 2000
BRANDFORD BOASE AWARD

0 440 864194

CORGI YEARLING BOOKS

BROOKSIE
by Neil Arksey

Imagine being the son of one of England's top strikers . . . Great, yes!

No! Not if, like Lee Brooks, your dad – 'Brooksie' – has suddenly lost form and become the laughing-stock of the whole country.

Lee hates Brooksie for letting him down. And Lee hates having to move to a grotty new home without his dad. With his own on-pitch confidence at an all-time low, he even begins to hate *football*. But then he meets Dent and his mates and the chance is there for him to play again – with a team of seriously talented players. They've just one problem – no pitch!

A cracking football tale, filled with goal-scoring action and dramatic matchplay moments.

0 440 863813

CORGI YEARLING BOOKS

All Transworld titles are available by post from:

Bookpost, PO Box 29, Douglas, Isle of Man, IM99 1BQ

Credit cards accepted. Please telephone 01624 836000,
fax 01624 837033, Internet http://www.bookpost.co.uk
or e-mail: bookshop@enterprise.net for details

Free postage and packing in the UK. Overseas customers:
allow £1 per book (paperbacks) and £3 per book (hardbacks)